THE GIRL AND THE DEADLY EXPRESS

A.J. RIVERS

CHAPTER ONE

HIM

EIGHTEEN YEARS AGO...

I t was never supposed to be this way.

He had everything in place. His life and hers were tailored to align. It was what was meant to happen. What was written out in the book of life. Blood and stardust and mothers' milk formed into words that told their story. It was transcribed for them: laid out before them from the beginning. Her eyes shared their common past and in them, he saw his future. Drinking breath from her cupped hands would fill him with life. Give him immortality. As long as she breathed, he breathed. As long as their blood continued, he continued.

But it was never supposed to be this way.

Years were taken from him. From them. Those days were gone, dissolved away. All the possibilities of what could have been were set aflame. Injustice and the cruelty of others had reduced it to ashes. But he wasn't going to give up. He would rise above, pull her from the ashes. Create something new. In the scars of what was left behind, they would find their beauty.

He didn't know if he needed to forgive her. In all these years they spent apart, she never even glanced his way, never murmured his

1

name. She never displayed what was truly in her heart. But he knew it was there. At the very core, buried where only Creation could hide and protect it, she held him. She held what they shared and what they would always share. Maybe it wasn't her fault she'd lost sight of it. She had been misled, lured away from him by a pretender. Familiar eyes and a Cheshire smile. It was hard to pull away when it seemed so right.

It was up to him to help her. His mind was clear, his thoughts precise. He could see sharply through her confusion. She would know. He would reach within her and find what was hidden, draw it out, and show her. When there was no choice, when the fog was gone, she would see him.

Maybe it was better this way. He hadn't thought about that. In the years that dragged on and the days that burned around him, he could only think of the pain and the injustice. The blank slates around him were torture. He could only let his mind etch them with the images of what slipped through his fingers. Every day the images grew, a thicket of vines devised of his imagination and studded with glass flowers. They bloomed and shattered, slicing deep until blood ran and tinted his vision red. It was all he could think about. It was the only way he could venture beyond the walls to where he was supposed to be and watch as what they created became reality.

Those walls were gone now. He emerged from the shards, and through the blood, he was purified. He could let go of the torment and see how it strengthened him. It only made his love deeper. It only proved his truth. Those trials and tribulations were what needed to be done to show his worth and sharpened his focus. Now he was ready. He would show her all he did for her, and she would be ready for the sacrifice. Then what was his and had been stolen would be restored. What was theirs and had been held away would be restored. Only then could they truly thrive.

Keeping the distance between them had been brutal. Another trial to prove himself. But it was his only choice. He had been cast out, tossed aside. Stricken from memory. But the erasure could never really be complete. Nothing could filter blood and empty minds. They could pretend. But he was there. He had always been there. He would always be there.

It was never supposed to be this way.

Yet it was and there was nothing he could do to change it now. Those days were gone. Those heartbeats were counted. He couldn't have them back. But he could have the rest. He was cast aside, just like all the righteous. They clawed through and bore the pain to emerge powerful and anointed, and that was what he would do. He would prove himself to her. He wouldn't let anything stand in his way. He would do what needed to be done to protect her and ensure she was never taken from him again.

It was never supposed to be this way.

But it wouldn't be again. She would be his everything. Always.

CHAPTER TWO

I'm not sure why people bring flowers to the hospital. I can almost understand potted plants, but even that feels strange. *I'm sorry you're not feeling well, here's the obligation to sustain the life of another being.* Cut flowers are completely beyond me. They're lovely, don't get me wrong. I love a good whiff of a rose as much as the next person. But it has always felt out of place and even a little morbid to walk into a hospital room with a handful of flowers chopped from their stems and slowly dying as a means of cheering someone up.

Maybe it's an issue of perspective.

But that's why the roses I'm holding as Sam and I walk into Pamela's hospital room are shimmery and metallic, their red just a little too red and their thorns a mediocre little flick of black ink. Her eyes lock on them as soon as she sees them, and one dark blond eyebrow arches up.

"What are those?" she asks.

Her voice is gradually working its way above a strained whisper. She only winces slightly when the words push past the row of stitches

5

across her throat. My hand shoots out toward her, presenting her with the bouquet.

"Dark chocolate," I tell her. "With those little crispy rice doodads."

"I do enjoy a doodad," Pamela says, accepting the flowers and peeling back a corner of red foil to reveal some of the chocolate.

"Can I get you some water for those?" Sam asks.

"Well, chocolate really does go better with wine, but I don't think the doctors are going to let me have a vase of cabernet for a while."

"How are you feeling?" I ask. "I know that's kind of a stupid question, considering, but it's the social contract. I ask; you lie."

Pamela manages a smile. "I'm actually doing better. Still hurts, but it's healing. No infections, so I'm grateful for that. It could have been a lot worse."

"I'm sure this is going to come out sounding a lot different than I intend it to… but I'm glad Sarah's knife was so sharp," I tell her.

She laughs, then cringes. "I appreciate the sentiment."

The truth is, the fact that Sarah Mueller used an extremely sharp knife when she slit Pamela's throat in that cemetery is the only reason Pamela is still alive. If it was dull, it could have mangled the flesh and torn apart the blood vessels and arteries so much they couldn't have been pieced back together. Pamela only lived because of the combination of a very sharp blade and a last-second movement that let the knife slice cleanly through. The smooth cut made it possible for the doctors to stem the bleeding and piece her back together.

The same couldn't be said for Sarah. After everything she put Sherwood through, all the lies and deceit, murder and a gunshot victim, everything just to try to discredit me, all she had to show for it was a bloody death on a stranger's grave. My bullet tore through her in the instant after she cut Pamela's throat. She was dead in the next.

It was too good for her. I know I shouldn't say that about another human being, especially after everything I've done to try to save lives. But it might be because of everything I've done that makes me say that.

Sarah was so focused on her perception that I destroyed her life by having her boyfriend arrested for murder, she couldn't think of anything but bringing me down. She genuinely believed if she could make me look like I had lost touch with reality and my crumbling mental health had become dangerous to the people around me, Travis Burke would be given a new trial for the murder of his wife. A murder that became my first case with the FBI. The complicated, disturbing chain of events created by that belief left a young woman dead, an innocent man struggling with a gunshot wound, my new friend in the hospital, and a town of shattered lives.

And it almost worked. Not that it would have ever led to the Burke case being reopened. That evidence was indisputable, and in the years that have passed since proving his involvement, Burke went on record more than once talking about his wife's murder. It would have done nothing to benefit either of them, but Sarah still almost turned the entire town of Sherwood against me. Her twisted game of stealing the name and story of Pamela's cousin to create a neighbor no one believed I met nearly ruined my life. She nearly stripped me of my reputation, my job, my relationship with Sam, and my future. And not only had my time in jail and public ridicule nearly broken me down, had I not fought with every fiber of my being, she would have cost Pamela her life as well. It was poetic justice Sarah Mueller, died on the grave of the woman she used and defamed to torment me.

"Kevin had his second hearing today," Sam tells Pamela.

I wait for the emotion. I'm honestly not sure which one it's going to be. There are several different options for how she could react to the man who betrayed her. He said he did it for her, but we all knew Kevin really teamed up with Sarah to save his own ass. She dangled the juicy gossip of his affair with Pamela in front of him and threatened to toss it to his wife like a piece of meat to the lions. It likely would have ended much the same way for both him and Pamela. The only way to keep her mouth shut was to do exactly what she said, which amounted to accomplice to murder. And attempted murder, if we could prove he really did try to run Pamela off the road the day of the poisoning.

"What happened?" she asks, her face like stone.

There's the Pamela I know.

7

"A lot of arguing. Legal mumbo jumbo, essentially. Because Sarah is dead, there's no one for him to inform on to make a plea. Prosecutors don't really care if he can spill everything about a dead woman. But his attorneys are arguing he shouldn't be held culpable for Nicole Bowman's death because of Sarah's hold over him. The whole thing could go one of three ways. It could either get really nasty and drag on for months or even years. They could offer him a plea based on what they can prove his level of involvement was with the totality of the crimes. Or they could come to the conclusion he wasn't responsible and drop all charges against him. I highly doubt it will end up as the third option," I explain.

"I hope not. He deserves at least something," Pamela tells me. Apparently, Pamela's good will toward him has worn off, the more she healed.

Sam and I stay a little longer, then leave Pamela to her painkiller drip and an afternoon of trashy TV in between naps. Her hospital stay shouldn't last too much longer. A couple more days and the doctors will send her packing, but for now, she needs the rest.

We stop by Pearl's Diner on the way back to my house. Pearl Holloway looks older these days. Not that anyone blames her. She's probably faring far better than most people would after going through what she did. I'm sure she thought the mass poisoning and murder of Nicole Bowman at her diner would be the worst thing she could weather, but she was wrong. Now she faces the reality that her grandson Kevin was at least partly responsible and is trickling his way through the justice system.

But Pearl is a strong woman. A throwback to another time when people had the fortitude to get through and the perseverance to want to. She's keeping her head up and her business open. I know one day soon, the crowds will come back. The whispering will stop. One day it will all be back to normal. Until then, I keep stopping by for a hug and lunch. It might be a while before I'm able to stomach biscuits and gravy or chocolate cake, but for now, the turkey club with a side of potato salad and slabs of lemon bars will do me just fine.

Rather than staying at the Diner, we bring our food back to my house and sit in the living room. Cold weather always makes me want to be home. The promise of a cold December is certainly nipping at my nose.

"Were you able to get in touch with Creagan?" Sam asks.

He scoops up some of his potato salad with a house-made potato chip. One of Pearl's specialties.

"That's an aggressive potato-eating approach you've got going there," I observe.

"It gives me all the textures," he offers with a grin.

The small home gym he has in the back room of his house is a wonder of body-sculpting technology. He eats like that and still manages to have a body that would be right at home in art history books.

"Anyway. Yes, I did talk to Creagan. He wants to have a conference so we can get everything officially worked out," I tell him, plucking the toothpick out of one half of my sandwich, so I can take a bite.

"How does that make you feel?" he asks.

I slide my eyes over to him and shake my head. "Nope. None of that. I've had enough of that. My personal growth might have brought me to a place where I'm willing to admit therapy can be beneficial, but I'm still not into people tiptoeing through the tulips of my mind. Not about this, anyway. Other stuff, maybe sometimes. But this... this, I've got under control."

"So, you're positive about this? You're sure this is what you want?" he asks.

"If I wasn't, it's not what I would be doing."

"When are you meeting with him?"

"He says he's not going to have time until after the holidays. We'll put something together then," I tell him.

"So, you have time to change your mind."

"Are you afraid I'm going to?"

"Are you going to?"

I put down my sandwich and reach out to take Sam's hands.

"Listen to me," I say. "I've thought about this a lot, and this is what I want. The FBI has always been my dream, and it still is. But that

9

doesn't mean I have to be right there near Quantico. It doesn't mean I have to be in the headquarters all the time. Plenty of agents live and work in other places."

"It hasn't always been your dream," he points out.

I let out a breath. When he looks at me, Sam still sees the girl he knew when we were growing up in Sherwood. The teenager he fell in love with so long ago. The high school sweetheart. The girl with the paintbrush in her hand and ink stains on her fingers. It's been a long time since I've looked inside myself and seen that girl.

"It's my dream now. But I can follow it in a different capacity from Sherwood," I tell him. "Can't you be happy about that?"

He leans forward and kisses me. "Yes. I can be happy about that."

CHAPTER THREE

I t didn't feel like Thanksgiving a couple of weeks ago when Sam mentioned it. The cold was in the air, and the leaves had already turned brown and made their way down to the grass, but the feeling just wasn't there. It still isn't. Not really. Not the way it used to be. Thanksgiving always used to be one of my favorite holidays. Possibly my favorite. But this year, I just can't find that feeling, that nostalgic tug in my belly that always used to come when I thought about things like turkeys and cornucopias and the Macy's day parade.

Not that I'm not thankful. If anything, I'm more thankful this year than I have been in most other years in recent memory. There's no shortage of things for me to feel thankful for and grateful about. Not the least of which is simply being alive to see another Thanksgiving. But there's an almost flat feeling to it this year like I never got the running start I needed earlier in the fall to make the big leap into the holiday season.

The situation with Sarah didn't help. Actual Thanksgiving got swallowed up by the case and its aftermath, so Sam and I didn't even celebrate. But we're making up for that today, and in a few hours, Bellamy and Eric will be at my house looking for turkey. I'm determined not to let my holiday funk get everyone else down. I'll fake the

Norman Rockwell cheer with the best of them. Maybe it will even convince me. Maybe all it's going to take is jiggling a memory somewhere, like everything that's happened in the last few months has clogged up my mind, and I just need to shake something free so the Thanksgiving feelings can come back.

"Happy Thanksgiving!" Sam bellows from the living room.

I walk out of my bedroom still in a bathrobe and slippers and discover the man I'm dating, a man I very well might love, resplendent in brown and gold. The sweater is straight off the cover of a Sears catalog in the late eighties, and the football he has clutched in one hand has bad idea written all over it.

This is helping.

"You certainly are cheerful this morning," I grin.

He comes up for a kiss, and I notice he already smells like warm bread. Which means somewhere he's packing a tray or two of rolls. Those don't come out very often. They were his grandmother's specialty when we were young, and they got passed along to him because he had no sisters to carry the tradition. I don't know what's in them. It's a closely guarded secret shared only with those who enter the inner sanctum of the Johnson family. My extensive experience and expert knowledge can only deduce it has something to do with yeast, butter, and maybe cocaine. They're that addicting.

Sam transforming into a Hallmark movie hero, sparks some of the holiday feelings in me. I get myself dressed so we can start dinner. The impeccable timing of my two best friends means they show up at the door just as I set the bowl of mashed potatoes on the table. They come in with bright smiles and bearing side dishes and desserts. It's good to see them, and I let myself drift away into the warmth, good food, and candlelight. It starts to fade the corners of my thoughts and buff them away like watercolors until I'm not thinking about anything else. We become that portrait, that perfect holiday that winds up as the frozen image of an entire year, an entire time in your life.

But it isn't long before Bellamy brings me back down to Earth. We've finished eating and are carrying massive wedges of pumpkin pie into the living room. As I go to curl up in the corner of the couch where I always sit, I notice Bellamy's leather satchel. I go to move it, and her eyebrows shoot up like she's just remembered it's there.

"Oh," she gasps. "I can't believe I didn't show these to you yet."

"What is it?" I ask as she sets her plate down on the coffee table and reaches for the satchel.

Sitting down beside me, she dips her hand into the bag and pulls out a handful of papers. It isn't documents like I'm used to her showing me from work, but folded papers and bits of stiffer card-stock. It takes me a second to realize I know exactly what it is.

"I have what Christina Ebbots gave me when I went to see her, and she also sent me a few other things she found from her dad. She said when she gets back; she'll look for more and send whatever she can find. She knows there's more," Bellamy says.

"What is that?" Eric looks over with a frown.

He takes a long sip of coffee, and I stare at him before glancing back at Bellamy.

"You didn't tell him?" I ask. She shakes her head, so I continue. "It's letters and postcards from my mother."

"To whom?"

"Charles Ebbots. The man who owned the house where they lived," Bellamy says.

"And where my mother died," I add, looking down at the postcard she sent me a scan of through email. "In theory."

"In theory?" Eric asks, sounding confused. "What do you mean?"

I look between them again. "You know, I'm really disappointed in the two of you. What good is having my two best friends pretend not to be wrapped up in each other if you don't even keep each other informed?" They both blink at each other, then at me, but I'm not buying it.

"Don't try the innocent looks with me. We're not going into the next year with all this will they-won't they. You've got about three weeks to figure this out." Three pairs of eyes continue to stare at me, and I sigh. "I'm sorry. That was a lot."

"It's alright," Sam says comfortingly. "Every Thanksgiving's got to have a drunk uncle who gets belligerent. This year, it's you. And since it's actually December, you can be the drunk Thanksgiving uncle and put a down payment on drunk Christmas uncle as well."

Bellamy lets out a quiet cheer and waves her hand like she's holding a pennant. I manage a hint of a laugh, but it can't be much more than that. The words and images I'm holding in my hands are gradually stitching my throat closed. I hold the postcard out to Eric.

"This postcard was written by my mother. April 17, 2003. The Thursday before Easter. It talks about us spending Easter in Vermont that year," I explain.

"You never told me you spent time in Vermont," he says.

"That's part of the problem," I nod.

"Part of?"

"I'll be right back." I go into my bedroom and pull out my fireproof chest from under the bed. I take the papers out of it and bring one back into the living room to show Eric. "This is my mother's death certificate."

"April 17, 2003," he reads. I nod and point to the top of the page, indicating the state that issued the certificate. "Florida."

"Now you're beginning to see the problem. How could she have mailed a postcard at the top of the East Coast and died at the bottom? The postcard is postmarked on that Thursday, which means the earliest it could have been left at the post office is still after five on Wednesday."

"Right, because any earlier and it would have been postmarked on Wednesday," Eric notes, stroking his chin.

"Exactly. My mother died just before one in the morning."

"So, she would have had to drop off the postcard and travel all the way from Vermont to Florida in about seven hours," Eric muses.

"Unless she dropped the postcard off in a sidewalk mailbox earlier," Bellamy points out. "Sometimes, those aren't emptied out until evening, but she could have put it in hours before."

"Sure," I say. "That would give her more time to travel from Vermont to Florida, but it doesn't explain one thing."

"What?" Eric asks.

"She wasn't in Vermont. She was home in the days leading up to her murder. The whole time. She was supposed to leave that night. I thought she had left. Right up until they wheeled her body out, I thought she wasn't home," I say.

"She was supposed to leave that night?" Eric asks. "You never told me that."

"It's not something I think about much. I don't know why she didn't leave or what happened. All I know is that night she was supposed to be traveling to New York to meet up with some friend who had come in from Russia. Her flight was at midnight. She was going to be back for Easter," I explain.

"Then how did a postcard from her get sent from Vermont?" Eric asks.

"And how did she end up dead at home almost an hour after she was supposed to be on an airplane?" Bellamy asks.

"I don't know."

CHAPTER FOUR

"You didn't know about any of this when you were younger?" Eric asks.

I shake my head. "No. I didn't even know who owned the house we lived in until Bellamy found all this out. It was never mentioned."

"Did you look into the death certificate?"

"Remember when I went to Florida a couple of weeks ago?" Bellamy asks.

Eric's eyes snap to me, then back to her. "I thought you said you were going on vacation."

"I was. I did. There was plenty of vacationing. There just also happened to be some investigating. And I happened to have a look into the death certificate. The department of vital statistics wouldn't give me any information, but I poked around and found Emma's mother's obituary. That sent me to a funeral home where there was supposedly a viewing."

"Supposedly?" he raises an eyebrow.

"My mother was cremated," I explain. "She didn't want any of that pomp and circumstance surrounding her death. It was one thing I really remember about her. She always said she didn't want there to be a bunch of people standing around, staring into a box at her and crying. When her life was over, she just wanted to be cremated and have everyone keep living. I hated it. I hated the thought of her being cremated and not even having the finality of a funeral or anything. It felt like we were just forgetting her. But my father wasn't going to do anything she didn't want."

"Is it possible he did and just didn't tell you? Maybe he did have a viewing, but kept you away from it to protect you since you were so young?" Eric asks.

"No. I was with my father every second for weeks after she died. I could barely stand to be in a different room than him for more than a couple of minutes. I dragged my sleeping bag into his room and slept there. He didn't go to work. The only time I wasn't right there with him was the day after she died when he had to go to the police station. That was only for a few hours, and I watched him get into the police car and then come back in it. She didn't have a viewing," I insist.

"The funeral home wasn't exactly forthcoming with me, but I did find something while I was there," Bellamy adds.

She tells him about the employee telling her about the man who came to ask about my mother and finding my ex-boyfriend Greg's name in the guestbook. Eric's eyes flash.

"And you didn't tell me any of this?" he demands. "I'm investigating a bombing that may or may not have to do with a missing man, and you don't tell me when you find his name written in a funeral home guestbook?"

"I'm not a part of that investigation," I point out. "You might remember a bit of a snit I had with Creagan over it. He, in no uncertain terms, told me I was to have nothing to do with investigating Greg or the bombing. I wasn't even supposed to think about him."

"That doesn't mean you ignore when you find potential evidence of where he's been and what he's been up to! You know that, Emma. You might be here playing house, but you're still a federal agent."

"Hey," Sam warns, holding out a hand to stop Eric. "That's enough."

"Don't talk to me like that," I say to Eric. "This has nothing to do with you."

"It has everything to do with me. You might have been locked out of the bombing investigation and told to stop trying to track down Greg because you keep interfering, but that doesn't mean you can just cut the rest of us out when it suits you. It's still your responsibility to bring anything potentially pertinent to an investigation to the attention of the team."

"Interfering?" I sputter incredulously. "That's such bull. You're the one who came to me to show me the video of him in the bus station before the bomb went off. And if it wasn't for me, you wouldn't know anything about the recording from Mary's laptop."

Realization hits me like a punch in the middle of my chest. "Oh, my god."

"What?" Sam asks. "What is it, Emma?"

My eyes lock on Bellamy. "The name."

"The name?" she asks. "What do you mean?"

I run to the desk at the side of the room and pull out a pad of paper and a pen. Bringing it back to the coffee table, I write down the name 'Mary Preston' and put the piece of paper on the table.

"Mary Preston. That's the name of the vlogger who was killed in the bombing. It was her video that had Greg on it, giving something to the man at the information desk and mentioning me. A video that no one should have had access to," I explain. "And as far as I know, there's still no one who knows how it was sent."

I look to Eric for confirmation. He's still angry, but he shakes his head.

"No. They're still trying to figure it out."

"Alright. Look at her name. Mary Preston. Now, look at my mother's death certificate. It lists her maiden name as well as her married name."

I slip the certificate across the table to line up with the piece of paper so Bellamy can look at both names at the same time.

"Mariya Presnyakov," Bellamy murmurs.

She pronounces it like 'Mariah', and I shake my head.

"No. It's Russian. It's pronounced like 'Maria'," I tell her.

"Like 'Mary'," Sam says.

"Yes. You look at those two names, and it looks like someone tried to take my mother's name and change the Russian to English."

"What does that have to do with anything?" Eric asks.

I narrow my eyes at him. "Seriously? You just threw a temper tantrum because I didn't immediately fill you in on everything that happened that may or may not involve Greg, and you can't even see it? The name written in the guestbook was Greg's, but it wasn't. Mary's name is like my mother's, but it's not. They are too close to be a coincidence."

"If it's not a coincidence, what does it mean?" he asks.

"I don't know, but someone knew that recording of Greg's voice was on Mary's video. They knew how to access it on the cloud and how to send it to me. That's not an accident," I point out. "I didn't tell you about Bellamy finding Greg's name in the guestbook because I don't want my family dragged into the Bureau's investigation of the bombing. We don't know who wrote his name or why. But the connection is there somewhere. You were willing to help me once, Eric. You need to decide now if you're going to keep helping me."

"You have to promise me you're not going to do anything that might compromise the bombing investigation," he counters.

"I can't promise that because I don't know how any of this intertwines. All I can do is promise when I find those threads, I'll tell you. You just have to promise me in return that you'll let me be the one to pull them. I'm at the center of all this, and I'm going to be the one to unravel it."

"You just make sure I know what's going on. A lot of people lost their lives that day."

"I don't need you to lecture me, Eric. I understand the gravity of this. Possibly more than anyone. And if I can figure out what it all means, I can get justice for those families. And for me."

—————

A few hours later, Bellamy and Eric have headed back, but I'm still perched in the corner of the couch, a half-eaten pie beside me. It's not my first slice. It won't be my last. Sleep isn't going to catch me tonight.

"Did you figure anything else out?" Sam asks.

A mug of coffee appears in front of my face, and I take it gratefully.

"I'm just trying to understand it. Why would she fake an Easter postcard to make it look like we were in Vermont? And if that one isn't real, what else was she lying about when she wrote to this Ebbots guy? I keep looking at these letters and wondering which of them are fake, too," I sigh. "I just don't get it."

"Does anything else stand out to you? Anything you can pinpoint in those letters that don't match up to what you remember?" he asks.

Sam sits down beside me on the couch and rests his hand on my leg. I've long since shucked the Thanksgiving dinner-appropriate clothes I was wearing in favor of sweats, and the warmth and familiarity of his touch through the fabric is soothing.

"That's the thing. I don't know. There's so much of my childhood I don't really remember or that I'm not sure about. And I think that was on purpose," I say.

"What do you mean?"

"It's hard to explain, but it's like things were done to keep me back a step. Like my parents, and especially my father, never wanted me to really know what was happening or what was coming next. I'd wake up one day and we're moving three states over. And then a month later we're moving back. And then they'd leave for mysterious trips. Or I'd be sent to the Sherwood house with my grandparents. I never knew what to expect. So there are things in these letters I'm not entirely sure about, but I don't know if that's because they didn't happen or I just don't know."

"Why would he do that?" Sam asks.

"I always assumed it was to protect me, but sometimes I wonder if it wasn't about me at all. Maybe I was just along for the ride. And the thing is, there's more. Bellamy says Christina Ebbots told her she's sure there are a lot more somewhere in the house, but she won't be able to look for them until she's back after the holidays."

"So, don't focus on that. You have no control over what else she might have. Think about what she sent you and if it means anything."

I show him the picture in my hand. "This was in one of the letters."

He takes it and looks down with a smile. "They're so young. You look just like your mother."

It makes my heart swell, and tears sting the backs of my eyes. She was the most beautiful woman I ever saw. Even to this day, I've never seen a woman more striking than her.

"She was a lot younger than me here," I tell him. I flip the picture over to check the inscription on the back. "1986. She was twenty."

I turn it back over and start to mention the shirt she's wearing, one I distinctly remember in the sea of vague memories of my childhood. Then something hits me, and I stop. Flipping the picture back over, I stare at the inscription again.

"What?" Sam asks. "What are you looking at?"

I hold the picture out to him. "Look at the inscription. I thought it said 'M and I. Mariya and Ian."

"Your parents' names," Sam says, nodding.

"Right. But look at the second letter. Is that an 'I'? Or is it a 'J'?"

CHAPTER FIVE

HIM

EIGHTEEN YEARS AGO...

"**A**re you absolutely confident?" he asked, staring into the dark eyes looking back at him.

There was no light in those eyes. There hadn't been for a long time. It was offered up in sacrifice for power and indulgence, satisfaction, and control. Xavier nodded silently.

He didn't know how Xavier found the information, but he didn't care. All that mattered was he found it. The chase was over now. For so long, he had been running, searching, waiting. There were times when he got so close; it was almost in his hands. He felt the warmth of her against his skin and breathed in the smell of her until she seeped into every fiber of him. But then it was taken again. He carried on. He forced himself forward. Step in front of step. Feet against the ground, soul against the world.

She was a part of him. Even when she was pulled away. Even when he had to step back and let her go for a time. He always knew it wouldn't last forever. They would come back together. She was part of his essence. Inextricable from him. No matter what it took, he would draw her back, exactly as she should have been. They never should have been apart. If all had worked out the way it was meant to, the way he wanted it to before he had to humble himself and submit to the tribulation that proved himself, they would have already shared so many years together.

He would never be able to get back those years. Sometimes the thought of that drove him mad. The torment would creep into the sides of his mind and up the back of his neck until it invaded his thoughts. Those were the moments when he almost lost control. When he risked letting go of everything he held onto so tightly. He could lose everything because of that despair. He couldn't let that happen. He had to restrain himself. Remind himself he was more than that. He was stronger, smarter, worthier. All he went through only increased his strength. When it was finally time for him to eliminate all that stood in his way, everything he went through would be worth it.

She was worth it. She was worth everything. And now he would never have to long for her again. He knew where to find her.

Levi and Thomas waited just where he told them to. They didn't know what to expect from him. This wasn't the first time they stood ready. It wasn't the first time they prepared themselves to go to war. But they were willing to do whatever he asked of them. They could already see his power.

It would take time for him to climb through the ranks, to rise to the surface. But he would. A day would come when he would be above them all. It took time to create a god of chaos, but when his time came, he would humble the world. Knees would bend, or they would break. Either way, they would bow.

These two understood. Levi and Thomas were loyal to him. They would do as he asked, knowing the rewards their service would bring. If they pleased him, they would be favored. That would mean everything to them. And his favor would carry them far. They wouldn't languish among the lowest ranks. They wouldn't have to grapple for attention and hope for another to notice them. Their lives would be more than just endless toil.

For others, that toil was all they could hope for in the mission.

There were the grains of sand, and there was the sea. Leviathan needed both. And when the crashing of powerful waves consumed the sand, there was always more to replace it.

"I have the address," he told the waiting men.

Their shoulders squared, and their chests lifted as if the words filled them. This is what they had been waiting for. Many other times they'd been called. They stood ready, right on the precipice of greatness. But it was always taken away. They never had that chance to fulfill the promise. Now they were another step closer.

"You cannot hesitate. There will be cameras. There may be lookouts. Keep your eyes open and pay attention to what's around you. When there is an opening, you have to move. Stopping even for an instant could reveal you. Make it fast and make it clean. As soon as it is done, you leave. Go in a different direction than you came. If anyone heard you, they will be looking on that path. Don't stop for anything," he instructed them firmly.

"What about proof? Should we take a picture?" Levi asked.

"There's no need. I will hear soon enough. It matters more for you to get out." He looked between them, meeting their eyes intently. "And if you're found?"

"We won't be," Thomas said without hesitation.

He gave a single, slow nod. It was exactly as he wanted to hear it. As they walked away from him, he felt a sense of peace fill him. There would be blood, but with blood came order. Blood cleansed. Blood redeemed. Blood paid debts. Blood sharpened minds and brought hands to action. And this blood would release chains and return what was rightfully his.

There wasn't long to wait now. No more years. No more months. Soon. Soon it would be over.

CHAPTER SIX

NOW

"Considering a new look?" Sam raises an eyebrow as he sits down beside me on the couch and peers over my shoulder at my computer screen.

I glance at him, and he holds out a white Styrofoam cup.

"Is that one of Pearl's peppermint shakes?" I ask.

"Would I bring you anything else in a white cup three days before Christmas?" he responds.

Snatching the cup from his hand, I eagerly suck down some of the intensely thick shake. It's pure candy cane on my tongue and smooth going down my throat. These shakes were always one of the few things I carried with me from Sherwood during the long years I stayed away. I didn't let myself think of the town or anything in it very much, but when the holidays rolled around, Pearl's peppermint shakes were never far from my mind.

After getting down a few sips, I point to the screen.

"Mary Preston," I tell him.

Sam nods and takes the cup from my hand to steal a sip.

"Pairing metallic eyeshadow with your regular daytime rotation?" he asks, reading the title of the video.

"Apparently, it adds pop and visual interest to even your most toned-down look," I say, reading off some of the description. "But I'm not after the makeup tips."

"What are you after?" he asks.

I let out a sigh. "No idea. Whatever it is, I haven't found it. I've been going through all of Mary's videos, her social media, all the articles about her. Everything I can find that has anything to do with her, I'm looking through it trying to find anything that might explain the connection."

"You really think there is one?" he asks.

"There has to be. It's too convenient. Someone sent me that clip of the video. Which means they had access to Mary's cloud. How would they even know to look for it unless they already knew it was there? I've been going through all of her videos, trying to find patterns."

"Have you found any?"

"A ton of them. That's kind of the problem. She follows a formula. Every video she does is essentially the same structure, same approach. And there are at least two or three videos every week. Nothing has stood out to me in any of them so far," I say.

Before he can answer, the sound of a car door outside makes our eyes snap to each other. Setting my computer down, I cross to the large window at the front of my house and slide the curtains aside to peek across the street. A little more than a month ago, I stood just like this, watching through the window at what I thought was the murder of my new neighbor happening in the house across the street. Not long after that, it was Pamela's car pulling into the driveway that got my attention, which almost left me dead in the garage.

Now I know the house was empty, and both incidents were actually Kevin Holloway and Sarah Mueller drawing me into her web.

I don't know if that makes me feel better or worse when I see Pamela's red Miata pull up in front of the house again. Sam steps up beside me and puts an arm around my waist. He brings his mouth to my ear.

"Don't worry. I see her, too," he whispers.

I elbow him playfully in the side. "Too soon."

He laughs, and I pull on a coat and shoes before heading outside into the brisk December afternoon.

"Hey, Emma," Pamela calls out, waving from the front yard.

Sometime in the last few weeks, Lionheart Property Management finally put up a 'for sale' sign in front of the house. Even though the house had been on the market for many months, Derrick, the owner of the management company, hadn't put up a sign. He thought the signs looked tacky and took away from the appeal of the street. When a prospective buyer pulled up to the house, he didn't want them to see a property that was for sale. He wanted them to see their home.

The events of recent weeks have shifted his perspective on that a bit. At least for now. There might be a time when he decides to go back to his clandestine real estate approach, but for now, he's going with transparency.

"Good to see you out and about," I reply.

The scarf around her neck conceals her healing injury, and her full makeup and hair would distract anyone from knowing she had gone through what she did.

"It would be better if it was warm, but I'll take it. You actually saved me a trip coming over here," she smiles.

"I did?" I ask her, looking at her quizzically.

"I was going to come by and ask you to come to the house with me."

My eyes slide over the cold, empty windows at the front of the house and the door I once thought I saw smeared with blood.

"Haven't you gotten enough of this place?" I ask.

"You'd think. But it turns out I have some unresolved... stuff happening. The doctor thinks walking through the house might help me move past it," Pamela says.

I resist the urge to smirk. It wasn't too long ago she was taunting me for my own skirmishes with mental health. In fact, hers was a particularly forceful voice in the mob trying to oust me from Sherwood. It's a little taste of sweet reversal now knowing that she's the one on the couch. But considering everything she faced, I figure now isn't the time to get smug.

"That makes sense," I nod.

Pamela glances over at the house and lets out a breath before looking back at me.

"Would you come in with me?" she asks.

"Me?"

"You have a different perspective of all this than I do. When we walked through the house together the last time, I didn't know what was going on. I still thought you had..."

"Lost my marbles?" I finish with a smile, not wanting to slip back into the heavy feelings I've only just recently gotten out from under.

"At least most of the important ones. I didn't know if you were seeing things or making things up. I had no idea what you were actually going through. Now I do. I think it would be beneficial for both of us to go through it together," she explains.

I nod. "That makes sense." I glance back at Sam. "Want to come in?"

He shakes his head. "I actually just got a call from the station, and I need to go check it out." He comes up to kiss me. "I'll call you later. Be careful."

When his car is gone, I look at Pamela again. "I wish he wouldn't say that."

"Why?" she asks, starting toward the front door to the house.

I follow her, feeling tension creep up my spine the closer I get to the door.

"Because it's usually after he says it that things like getting locked in a garage with a running engine or falling down an elevator shaft happen," I point out.

Pamela's eyes flick up and down my body like she's evaluating me in a new light.

"Valid."

She takes a key from her pocket and uses it to open the door. Images flash through my mind as we step inside. I can still see the smear of blood that looked so real in the moonlight. I see the legs of who I thought was a woman named Ruby, battered and bloodied on the living room floor.

At the time, it was so intense, so real. Everything in me believed I just watched a woman who had become my friend get murdered. But only moments later when Sam arrived, all signs of the brutal killing were gone. The speed and smoothness of the orchestration was impressive, looking back, but the memory still makes my stomach turn.

"It's so quiet," I say.

"Tell me what you saw," she says. "I want to know what happened."

"There were boxes everywhere. Remember, she told me she was moving in, so there were things set up around like she was unpacking. When I think about that night, I can't honestly remember how much stuff there was. There were a lot of boxes and a few things, like a sweater hanging from the banister. I remember that because she wore dresses and sweaters all the time," I tell her.

"So did Ruby," Pamela murmurs. "At least, she did before she met... "

Her voice trails off. She doesn't want to say his name. The man who murdered her beloved cousin. That was the real Ruby. A woman who really did live and breathe. A woman who really did die at the hands of a man who once said he loved her. That made Pamela one of Sarah's victims well before she ever placed the knife against her throat.

I place my hand on Pamela's shoulder and give her a reassuring nod.

CHAPTER SEVEN

Pamela and I make our way slowly through the house, talking through it as we go from room to room. I never entered the house when I thought Ruby lived here. She always came to my house, so by the time I actually went inside, she was already gone. We go into the kitchen, and I see the oven again.

"When I came here to look around outside, there was sugar outside the door," I explain. "When Sarah came to my house to get sugar, she must have brought it back over here and just tossed it out. That really bothers me. I know that sounds ridiculous, considering everything else she did, but for some reason, thinking about her walking back over here and throwing the sugar out the back door really gets to me. She was just sitting there in my kitchen, bleeding her heart out to me. Now I know it was all an act. She thought of all that before she came to my house. Right down to the borrowing the sugar so she could pretend to bake a damn cake."

"She didn't think of it," Pamela whispers. "Not all of it, anyway. She stole most of it from Ruby."

A sheen of tears over her eyes expresses the painful depth Sarah's cruel game cut. The entire time I tried to convince the people around me, I saw the woman across the street, Pamela taunted me for losing my grip. She questioned my ability to do my job and the safety of having me be a part of police investigations. All the time, she had no idea the woman I met had stolen the identity of the cousin she was still mourning. It was part of the torment, part of the twisted way Sarah was trying to destroy my sanity and my reputation.

I resented her for it—and for her constant flirtation with Sam—for a long time. But these last few weeks have really put things in perspective for me. I never knew Pamela struggles the way she does. And ultimately, I signed up for a life of danger and fear. I've been shot at, chased, hit, and attacked more times than I can count. I throw myself into life-threatening situations as a hobby. Pamela doesn't. I can't blame her for still feeling shaken up. And even though part of me wants to feel glad now that the shoe is on the other foot and she's the one needing my help, I just can't. I feel bad for her.

We visit the attic last. This is the one room of the house we didn't go into when Pamela finally relented to showing Sam and me the house just after the faked murder. The smell of unfinished wood is strong, and I notice small dark spots on the floor to one side. Pamela gestures toward them.

"Fake blood," she says.

I nod. "Sam told me when they searched the house after the show-down in the cemetery; they found traces of fake blood and a couple things scattered on the floor. Kevin must have been waiting right out of view, and as soon as I went to call Sam, they brought everything to the attic. They knew people would be watching the house after that, so when they went to get everything out, they were rushing and must have dropped some things."

Pamela lets out a slightly shaky breath. "If I had let you come up here."

She says it almost like she thinks she's talking to herself.

"What?" I ask.

She looks over at me and shakes her head slightly. "Just thinking about the day we came here. After you saw... that. We didn't come up to the attic. I didn't see anything. I didn't notice anything strange, and I couldn't understand why you were still so determined something happened. Seeing everything that proved you were wrong should have snapped you out of it. The empty house, the new appliances. All of it. But it didn't change anything, and I just wanted to get out of the house. If we came up here, we would have seen that stuff. Maybe…"

I know where that thought's going, and I stop her. "It's not your fault. It wouldn't have stopped her. Even if we did come up here and find that stuff, all it would have done is proved someone was here. We wouldn't know who it was or why she was doing it."

She nods and wraps her arms around herself as she looks around the attic. Her eyes stop to the side, and she shivers.

"I really hope they looked in there," she says. "I know Derrick has shown this place a couple of times, but I don't want to be the one who shows it to the people who want to look in there and find a bunch of creepy stuff."

"What are you talking about?" I ask.

Pamela points across the attic, and I see a door I hadn't noticed before. "The closet. I hope the police went in there when they were sweeping the house. I know no one actually died here, but that doesn't mean I want to see the fake blood and stuff."

She shudders, but I'm fascinated by the door. "It's a closet? How big is it?"

"Fairly large. It's not really a closet, that's just how I think of it. Some of the people around here finished their attics and turned them into master suites with a nursery or dressing room. You should know what it looks like. Your house has one."

I pause at the door and turn to look at her.

"No it doesn't," I frown.

Pamela's head cocks to the side. "Yes, it does. Almost all the houses in this neighborhood were designed by the same team. They have different layouts, but one feature they share is the small room off the attic. It's a weird little quirk of this particular designer."

"He must have gotten over it by the time he got to my house, because there isn't one in my attic," I tell her.

"I know the layout of your house, Emma," she says.

My eyes narrow. "That's not creepy at all."

35

She sighs. "I've seen the plans. Remember, Lionheart manages your house. All that information is in the file, even if we're not actively handling the property. The original plans have the extra room just like all the other houses."

I turn back to the door and open it to peer into the small space beyond. "They must have changed their mind when they were building. That was my grandparents' house. I spent a lot of time crawling around in the attic when I was younger, and I know I would have noticed an extra room. That would have been my fort as fast as I could drag a blanket and bag of snacks up there. It's not there."

Pamela looks at me strangely, then shrugs.

"I guess it wouldn't be the first time a designer would change a feature in a house," she offers. "Especially if your grandparents didn't want it for some reason. The contractors might have just not built it but not bothered to change the plans."

I wouldn't have thought I would, but when we finish walking through the house and finally step back out into the cold, I feel relieved. Even though I already knew what happened, actually coming face to face with the empty house and seeing for myself how Sarah and Kevin managed to pull off what they did puts my mind more at ease.

For weeks, the world around me thought I lost grip on reality and questioned my sanity. I'd be lying if I didn't admit there were moments when I started wondering about it myself. In those moments, I knew what I was seeing and experiencing, but everything around me told me I was wrong. It was hard not to hear dozens of other people contradict me and hang on to the resolute belief in what was really happening.

Now would be the time for me to be grateful I'm stubborn as hell.

I call Sam as soon as I get back to the house.

"Everything okay at the station?" I ask when he answers.

"Yeah. Just a drunk causing trouble," he tells me.

I kick off my shoes and head toward the kitchen.

"Steven?" I ask.

Sam laughs. "This time, he stripped down to a pair of long underwear and started reciting a Christmas carol in the middle of the Square."

I pull open the refrigerator and pull out a container of last night's leftovers. Holding the phone between my shoulder and my ear, I grab out a bottle of flavored water and pop the door closed with my hip.

"Mark Twain or Muppets?" I ask.

"Neither, actually. Not A Christmas Carol the story. It was more a spoken word version of The Twelve Days of Christmas. He got all the way to the French hens before Savannah got to him."

"Got to give it to him for his dedication. So, why did they need you? Steven is usually pretty docile once you get a hold of him."

"The holiday season is bothering him, and he was a bit on the challenging side today. But we've got him nestled all snug in his bed... in the drunk tank," Sam explains. "How about you? How was the house tour? I have to admit; I'm still working on wrapping my head around you and Pamela not being at each other's throats."

"Me, too, a little bit."

Pamela and I have always had somewhat of a contentious relationship, even since high school. At least, she had a contentious relationship with me. Until I came back to Sherwood last summer, I didn't even give her a second thought. Then I found out she was fertilizing the grapevine with talks of me going fruit loops after a series of brutal cases. That's when I got in on the contention. But it turns out being dragged along by a sociopathic killer has a bonding effect.

I tell him about the house and the room in the attic. He brushes it off just as Pamela did, and I will myself to put it out of my mind. There's enough to think about without adding phantom rooms to the mix.

CHAPTER EIGHT

LAMB

Maybe he wouldn't survive this.

It wasn't a worry or even something to be afraid of. Just a thought. Just coming to terms with the reality.

That possibility didn't go through his mind in the first few days. Of course, then he didn't know what was actually happening. They made sure of that. Everyone around him played a game. Some didn't even know they were playing it. To them, it was life, their choice, and yet not. They didn't realize they were being orchestrated and being used to orchestrate others.

The way they were intertwined with each other was intentional, crafting a net of control around them. Whether they knew it or not, each was responsible for others, and others were responsible for them. The real weight hung on those who understood the manipulation because they knew they could never trust anyone around them. There was no way to know who was watching.

In those first days, he didn't know about any of it. But that was all the same control. It was the way it was devised. He wasn't taken or dragged away. Lotan convinced him to simply leave. With only the belief in a masked identity and a hidden name, he walked away. It didn't take long for him to learn the name Lotan or to understand what it meant, but it would take much longer, far longer than he would ever want to admit, to know the man behind it.

Lamb was a creature of habit. He always had been. From the time he was a very young boy, a schedule and consistent rituals controlled his every action. It took away questions and ambiguity, freeing him from the thousands of tiny choices and decisions put in front of other people every day of their lives. He didn't have to make those choices. They were already made for him.

Before his eyes even opened every day, he knew the time he would wake and the food he would eat. He knew what he would wear and the route he would drive. He knew where things were placed and what days he would take care of tasks like grocery shopping. In some situations, he even knew exactly what he would say.

These moments were already crafted for him, so he didn't have to come up with them. For some, that type of life would be restrictive and uncomfortable. To him, it was freeing. While he wasn't thinking about those things or making those choices, his thoughts could venture to other places and focus on other things. The only times he deviated were when duty and responsibility stood in the way. Doing what he was called to do would always come first.

And Lotan knew that. Somehow, he learned Lamb's ways. He used that knowledge to create a trap so invisible it took weeks for him to even know it was there at all.

At first, Lamb was honored to have been chosen and eager to do whatever he could to help with the mission. He had never heard of Leviathan, but confidentiality and classified projects were nothing new to him. He didn't know simply because he hadn't been told. As soon as he had, he was committed to it. He learned the name Lotan, a title that placed the man at the pinnacle of the project. Lotan was to be respected. Lamb already did. Before he ever looked into his eyes. Before he drove away with him. Before he performed his first task, he was already devoted because of the stories he was told.

Discovering the cracks was an accident. He wasn't looking, and the truth wasn't offered to him. Instead, it seemed to present itself. He couldn't help but follow it. That's when he first heard the name Lamb.

It was when he first watched everything he thought he was fighting for crumble away. Then he saw Lotan for what he was. It was like being a child seeing his favorite superhero, only to watch him peel away a mask and drop the cape to the floor.

A choice was put before him. Be a part of Leviathan or an instrument of Leviathan. The choice was his, and so were the consequences.

Now he wondered if he would make it out alive.

In many ways, it didn't matter. He made his choice. Neither.

It was incredibly risky what he was doing from within the control of Leviathan. Just like the crushing power of a maelstrom tumbling him around, the organization tried to swallow him, but he always managed to take that next breath. He wanted to escape, but Finn had a better chance. He did what he could, offering up the bits of information and telling him exactly how to leave them. It would unravel one day, and Leviathan would fall. Lotan would be forced to remove his mask and bow down.

But it took time. The process was extremely delicate and more dangerous with each passing day. As the foundation became less stable, the potential for disaster grew. He might not survive this. But he was willing to take that onto himself. What mattered was doing everything he could to protect Emma and to stop the destruction that could easily happen if Lotan was given the opportunity. One wrong move and many more would die.

All he could do was keep going and hope to slowly and carefully unravel the nets from the inside until there was nothing left to catch Lotan when he fell.

They called him Lamb. He had to prove he could also be the wolf.

CHAPTER NINE

NOW

"Christmas doesn't stand much of a chance around here, does it?" Sam comments as I push the lid of a green plastic tote into place and stack it on top of others in the corner.

"It's the second week of January. How much longer do you want me to keep the decorations up?" I ask.

He shrugs and reluctantly takes down a wreath he hung with clear fishing line from a hook in the ceiling just after our Thanksgiving. I think I remember that hook holding a potted plant when I was younger, but since I've been in the house, it's just been a random hook. Sam decided it needed a touch of holiday flair, and the strange floating wreath of festivity has been there since. But now it's time for that to get packed away with all the rest of the baubles and ornaments, tucked in the attic to wait for the next ten months or so.

"It was just nice to have you around for Christmas," he says. "It's been a long time."

I try not to let the guilt creep in. Now isn't the time for me to be thinking about the years that have passed. Everything we've missed together. I made the choice I did because it was what needed to be done, and I don't regret it. There are ways my life changed because of that choice, but it's the life I chose for myself. I would do it again.

Sure, I don't like to think about the time I spent without Sam, which is why I don't do it. If I let myself think about how life could have been different or where I might be now if I hadn't left him and Sherwood behind when I did, I might start questioning myself. And that's not something I'll let myself do.

The truth is, walking away from him all those years ago was painful as hell. It felt like tearing a piece of my soul out. But it was the pain that reassured me I was doing exactly what I was supposed to be doing. If it hadn't hurt that much, it would mean it didn't matter, and I really didn't have to leave in the first place. The reason I had to cut him off and leave my life behind was so I could devote myself entirely to what was ahead. Sam could never really understand that. I don't want him to. In order for him to understand the decision I made, he would have to understand the questions and the torment I've gone through every day. That's not something I would ever wish on him.

Those same questions and that same torment continue to hang over me even still. It always digs into me deeper at this time of year. It's why for years, there was no Christmas tree in my house; and why I did everything I could to avoid anything that seemed even close to festive and joyful at this time of year. After all the warmth of Thanksgiving, Christmas just feels empty and hollow. It's hard to really be in the holiday spirit when I don't have either of my parents with me.

I've spent seventeen Christmases without my mother. It's not lost on me that that means there have been more holidays in my life without her than there were with her. That doesn't make it easier. If anything, every Christmas is a little harder because it's another tacked on, and I know the number will never stop growing. As long as there are Christmases for me to celebrate, the scrolling record of the years she's been gone will just keep ticking up higher.

And every year I lose more. I'm adding years and losing memories. My father and I kept up with some of the Russian traditions my mother taught me when I was little, but they dissipated over the years. Now the smell of the roasted pork and strong broths she always made is only faint in the back of my mind. I can barely hear her singing her favorite songs. My forehead has lost the chilly feeling of her Christmas morning kiss, made frosty by spending the morning decorating the outside of the house with spruce.

More is going to fade away. I can't stop it. No matter how much I try to hold on to those holidays with her, time is going to buff them away. It's already started to do the same to the memories with my father. There have been fewer Christmases without him, but still enough to leave me missing pieces of my memories with him.

But it's not the same with him. Not yet. I don't know where he is or why there have been twelve Christmases without him. But nothing has proven to me yet there won't be more. That's what keeps me going; it reminds me that a life with the Bureau was my strongest choice. My only choice. I gave myself over to digging into the darkest shadows and bringing down the slimiest of criminals in hopes that one day I would know what happened to my mother. That I would know why my father left when he did. Those answers are more important to me than anything.

I pick up two of the totes and carry them up the narrow set of steps to the attic. I've been gradually emptying out the space since coming back here last summer. When I first moved back in, I didn't expect there to be anything up here. After all, the house had been used as a rental property for more than one family over the years. I didn't think anything that belonged to my grandparents would have been left behind. But instead of those families moving into an empty house, they came into a home still containing remnants of the family who spent decades there. My family. It surprised me to learn the renters were expected to live alongside lingering reminders of my grandparents, my parents, and even me.

There was more in the house when I got here, too. Decorations and strange collectibles that had been collected by nobody. Derrick from Lionheart Property Management wanted to offer a house that was already furnished and had the appeal of a lived-in home but without the emotional baggage that came with it being actually lived in. So random generic art took the place of my grandmother's paintings. Knick-knacks settled into place on furniture I'd never seen. All the personality of the house just painted over, only showing through in faint hints.

That's all gone now. Over the last few months, I've sifted those things out and replaced them with the old possessions out of the attic and the storage unit across town. The house is back to looking more like I remember from when I was younger. Right down to the Christmas decorations in the attic. And the smooth wall where Pamela says a door should be.

Sam comes up the steps behind me, and I move out of the way so he can stack the totes in the corner. He pauses beside me and looks at the wall where I'm staring. My home improvement projects haven't made it up here yet, so the walls are still slightly discolored from all the years of dust and age since the last time this place was freshened up.

"When I was really little, there was wallpaper up here," I tell Sam.

"Wallpaper?" he asks.

I nod. "It was never completely finished, but my grandmother put wallpaper up. I think it was used as a guest room. I don't remember it ever having beds in it or anything, but I used to come up here to read and play, and I remember there being wallpaper. There used to be a little table up against one of the walls that had a lamp on it too. I just figured it was being stored up here."

"So, your theory is your grandparents didn't want the extra little room built in the attic like was on the plans, but then they turned the entire attic into an extra room?" Sam asks.

His words are stretched out and thin, each one with a tenuous connection to the next. Like when you pull taffy and the pieces just barely stick together. He's trying to figure out the thoughts going through my mind, trying to follow along and unravel what I'm think-ing. That's become a habit of his since we've started working cases together. When he thinks I've come up with something, he starts trying to chase it.

I shake my head. "I don't have a theory. It's just an observation."

He nods. "Well, come on. There's still plenty of joy to suck out of the house."

I laugh and start to follow him down the stairs, but just before the room dips out of sight, I turn back to look at it. This has always been my grandparents' house in my mind. For the first time, I wonder what it was like before I knew it. Before they were my grandparents.

CHAPTER TEN

W hen we've finished packing away all the Christmas decorations, Sam drops down on the couch and rests his head against the back. I sit beside him, and he glances over to the side, catching sight of my laptop on the table.

"Are you still watching those Mary Preston videos?" he asks.

I let out a sigh and pull my computer into my lap. Swiping my finger across the mousepad wakes up the screen, revealing Mary's face paused in mid-sentence.

"I've watched them all at least a dozen times," I tell him. "I'm getting to the point where I can recite almost everything she says."

"And?" he raises his eyebrows with expectation.

"And I still don't care. I feel bad saying that considering what happened to her, but... I don't know; I just don't care about her opinions on winged eyeliner or her observations at the annual designer sample sale," I say.

"That's not what I was asking," Sam says.

"I know what you were asking." The cursor moves down to the comment section. "And my answer is still that I don't care. But that's the point. Why do you think these people do?"

The paused video disappears as I use the down arrow on my keyboard to scroll through the long list of comments.

"That's a lot of comments," he observes. I nod.

"And it just keeps going. There are hundreds of them. Some of her videos have thousands."

"Isn't that the point of being a social media influencer?"

"Yes, but what is she influencing? This isn't the Harvey Milk of our time we're talking about here. She's bubbly and can seemingly talk about anything endlessly. I'm sure there are plenty of boys in that teenager to early twenties demographic who enjoy looking at her," I tell him.

"I'm not following," he says.

"Interesting choice of words. That brings me to my next point. Mary was building up her platform. She hadn't quite made it to the big time yet, but she was definitely collecting followers. That's where most of her comments come from. Sometimes the same people would leave a dozen or more comments on the same video. They'll create threads with other people and try to engage with Mary. Look. You can see where she responds to some of them."

I point out several of the responses from Mary. "If you trace them from her very first video, you can see where some of her followers have really developed an attachment to her. Like they believe they are really her friends. Some of them can get really intense."

"Look at this one," Sam says, pointing out a particular name. "Pop-TartsandSoda. Nutritious."

"Breakfast of champions, and also one of Mary's most devoted followers," I say.

"I see that. She must have posted thirty times on this one video. She's having arguments with people over what they're saying about the video and about Mary. Do you think she knows her?"

"In real life?" I ask and shake my head. "No. There are comments on an earlier video of her basically spilling her life story to Mary and saying they should be friends. They live on opposite sides of the country. But I don't think she's who I'm looking for."

"Who are you looking for?" he asks.

"I'm not sure. But here's my thought. The person who sent me the video clip with Greg in it had to have close access to Mary. We've already established it wasn't her phone or her computer that were used to send it to me, that whoever it was had access to her cloud. So, what if it was one of these people?"

"One of her followers? You think they hacked her?"

"Maybe. But I don't think so. I think it's more than that. People like Poptarts over here are wrapped up in Mary. She is their focus. But that video clip wasn't about Mary. It was about me. Whoever sent it didn't care what she was saying or even that she was in the video at all. They only cared about Greg being there. Which means not only did they know who I was enough to recognize my name and find my personal contact information to share it with me, but they knew Greg, too. You heard that clip. The instructions to listen carefully were definitely needed. It was really hard to hear what Greg said because he was behind Mary and talking quietly."

"So, someone must have known to listen for what he was saying," Sam nods.

"Exactly. Even if it was just someone prodding around in her cloud, satisfying their post-mortem curiosity, why would they care about what Greg said if they didn't already know something about him? All he said was to give whatever it was to me. That's it. 'Give this to Emma Griffin'. Unless a person knew who Greg was and our relationship, there would be no reason for that to call any attention. Whoever sent that clip specifically went after the video for that clip. Which means it wasn't one of the people who are obsessed with Mary."

"Then why are you reading the comments?"

"Because they had to have access to her. It's not just about getting access to the cloud or to the video. Like you said, a hacker could have done that. My point is the intention. Someone would need to recognize the significance of that clip of video... or know it was going to happen," I tell him.

"Know it was going to happen? Greg has been missing for years. How could anyone possibly have known he would be at that bus station mentioning you?" Sam points out. "And if they did know, why would they go through Mary's vlog?"

I run my fingers through my hair and let out a breath. "All fantastic questions."

"What's this?" he asks, pointing at one of the comments. "One-thirty-four."

"It's a time-stamp. A specific point in the video," I explain.

"I understand what a time-stamp is," he tells me. "What I mean is, what is this one? Why is it in the comment?"

"Mary flips her hair. That's seriously it. She flips her hair over her shoulder. That same person comments on every one of her videos with time-stamps of when she flips her hair. Then at the end," I scroll to the bottom of the list of comments and point out the last comment left by the username JayCalhoun, "a smiley face. Every video. From her first one. Creepy, but that's why I'm not too concerned with him. I'll keep him on my radar, but again, he's too focused on her. He is here for Mary, and that's it. I'm looking for someone who doesn't fit in with the rest."

"Emma," Sam says, running his hand down my arm to get my attention. "Do you really think this has to do with your mother?"

"I do," I tell him. "It lines up too well."

"The names are similar, but your mother died years before you even met Greg. What would he have to do with her murder?" Sam asks.

I look back at the screen and the dizzying row of comments, usernames clamoring for a spark, a hint, a fragment of attention thrown their way by a girl in a video.

Betsy Marion
Jason McGregor
KnightandGay
Fredrick 'Slick' Mason
Dean Steele
MistyEyes
Jefferson West
Gray Parlor Photography

So many of the names repeat on video after video. Many show up a final time tacked onto the ends of previous videos, sharing memories and mourning. The voyeurism of the public grief makes my skin crawl. Lavish expressions of sadness and longing for this woman they didn't even know feels strange and out of place.

At the same time, I can't help but share in their sadness. Mary Preston was so vibrant and full of life in her videos. There've been times watching them when it slipped my mind, even for a few seconds, that she was no longer alive. And when it hits me, all I can see is the rubble of the bus station in Richmond.

"I think I need to go to Florida," I say. "That's where I last remember my mother. It's where she died and where all the confusion and questions keep going back to. I really think if I'm going to finally know why she was murdered, I have to figure out what happened afterward. If I can understand why there are so many conflicting stories and things that don't make sense, maybe I can work backward."

"When are you planning on going?" he asks.

"Soon. I want to wait until I can talk to Christina Ebbots. Bellamy set a good foundation for me, but I need to actually speak to her and find out what she knows about my parents or their relationship with her father. Maybe she'll have found more of the letters from my mother. I also want to ask her about the house and if she has any records of it."

"Why?"

"I don't remember how many times we stayed in that house or for how long. I thought we stayed in several different places in Florida, but the way she talked about it, it sounds like we kept going back to the same house. I want to know why. We traveled all over the place. Stayed in different states, different places within different states. Sometimes we bounced around from place to place in the same area in a matter of weeks. All that just so people wouldn't know where we were or be able to find us because of my father's work. But then we just go right back to the same house in Florida? It doesn't make sense," I explain. "She should be back in the next few weeks. I'll make plans after I see her."

CHAPTER ELEVEN

SEVENTEEN YEARS AGO...

She loved being in Florida no matter what the time of year, but there was something special about spring. In the days leading up to Easter, some places in the country still hid under the snow. Tiny green shoots and the occasional intrepid flower were starting to climb up through the crystals of ice and into the chilled air, but the last breaths of winter were unquestionably hanging on.

Not in Florida. Here the days of April were the first kisses of summer. While other people prepared to search for Easter eggs with chilly legs sticking out from their fancy dresses and flowers that hadn't broken through the surface yet, in Florida they were already laying out, tanning on the beaches in the hot sun.

The years she got to spend these weeks of spring in Florida were her favorite. She knew her Easter eggs would be nestled in bright green grass, and by the end of the day, she'd probably be tired and happy from hours spent splashing in the pool. It wasn't late enough in the year yet for the concrete to sting the bottoms of her feet, and the water was still bracing on her skin, but the promise was there.

Summer was coming. It almost felt like a secret. The crowds of people hadn't formed yet, and there were still times when it was almost quiet.

That year Easter felt a little different. She was still excited about it. She loved the bright colored eggs and the tiny treasures they held inside. She loved the basket she'd find at the end of the hunt and the chocolate bunny tucked among pink grass. Her mother always got the edible kind of grass rather than the crinkly plastic she could remember when she was a very little girl. She could still remember what the plastic grass looked like, how it caught the sunlight coming through the windows and splashed it's pink and shimmery reflection across the table and the white of her Easter dress. Her mother remembered what it looked like tangled in the brush of the vacuum cleaner and hanging from the corner of the cat's mouth.

She was still excited to celebrate, but she didn't know if she should be. That was the year she was turning twelve. Only three more months separated her from officially turning into a preteen. She didn't really know what that was supposed to mean, but it felt like it was going to change her. Like those months would pass, and suddenly there would be a shift in how she felt or looked or saw the world.

Suddenly she wouldn't be a child anymore. Maybe that started with Easter. Maybe she was getting too old to want to hunt for eggs through the yard or dig through her basket to discover all the little treats hidden there. Last year tiny bottles of nail polish and flavored lip balm replaced some of the toys she used to get.

No matter what ended up in her basket, she did have reason to be excited about Easter. It would mean her mother would be home. She hated when her mother traveled. She was used to her father traveling. He would be gone for days, sometimes a week or two. Then it was just her and Mama. She didn't worry about her father. He knew what he was doing, even when she didn't. And if Mama wasn't afraid, she wasn't going to be either. But she hated when Mama left. It wasn't as often as Dad. She stayed home most of the time. That only made it harder when she did leave.

She felt anxious knowing her mother was leaving that night and wouldn't be coming back until the night before Easter. She would be asleep when Mama left that night, and she would be asleep when she got back Saturday night. But when she got up Easter morning, Mama would be home. The family would be together.

She would run through the yard in bare feet looking for plastic eggs, then dye hard-boiled ones together. She'd sit in the pool of sunlight on the hardwood floor of the living room and open each egg, sampling the chocolate inside and making stacks of shiny coins she always found in them. They'd go into her piggy bank, the white one with her name painted across it, that her mother got at her baby shower when she was still pregnant. The whole house would smell like ham and brown sugar, potatoes and cabbage, coconut cake, and lemon meringue pie. Her mother's Easter blended with her father's, to make hers.

She was drawing each of them a picture to give them Easter morning. It was a surprise she'd been working on for the last few weeks, tucking the pictures away under her bed so her parents wouldn't see them before she rolled them up and stuffed them into the plastic eggs she kept aside just for them. One yellow, one purple. For Dad, for Mama.

That Wednesday evening, she did everything she could to stall going to bed. The longer she stayed awake, the shorter the time she would be away from her mother. They indulged her for a little while. After dinner, they curled up on the couch together and shared a bowl of ice cream while watching a movie. Even months later, she wouldn't remember the movie. All she would remember was the smell of a shower clinging to her mother's skin and the hint of bleach deep in the fibers of the white chenille blanket they cuddled up beneath. Her mother brought her to bed that night and tucked her in, reading her a few chapters from the book they were working on together. She was almost asleep when the bedside lamp went out, and the door to the hallway clicked closed. She stayed awake until she heard her mother call in another goodbye, goodnight, and a promise she would be back soon.

She didn't know anything else until the blue and red lights came through her window and drew her out of sleep. There was no siren.

That scared her. A siren meant they were trying. It meant they were doing everything they could. They wanted people out of their way so they could go as fast as they could to the people who needed their help. A siren meant hope. No siren meant there was nothing to do, no reason to try, no one to help.

The lights kept flashing long after she wanted them to stop. Minutes piled on top of each other. On the floor of the house beneath her, she could hear doors and voices. She got out of bed quietly, not wanting anyone to know she was there. But it wouldn't have mattered. There was so much happening in the entryway of the house; even if she had been loud, they wouldn't have noticed her. She wasn't what they were there for. She wasn't even on their minds. Somewhere in the back of her father's mind, she still existed. But only as a static image, lying in bed, sleeping. He didn't have to worry about her, so he didn't think about her.

At the top of the steps, the landing had closely placed spindles, perfect for her to hold and peer through. They offered her some sense of protection, shielding her from view if the people below just glanced up her way. The night air was chilly. She would remember that always. The day had been warm enough to lie in the grass and look up at the clouds passing through, but by the time she was curled up against her mother's side watching commercials for Easter candy and wishing time would slow down, the air had cooled. That wasn't so unusual. The days were warm during Florida springs, but as the hours passed, they weren't as able to hold onto the heat. Nights were often chilly enough for her to burrow under the covers and wish she was wearing socks.

That was the thought at the very edge of her mind as she sat on the steps and watched the men scurry around like ants below her. Her toes were cold, and she curled them up, digging them into the carpet that rippled down the steps from the landing at the top.

She didn't know what was going on. She wished her father would come find her, even if he was upset with her for getting out of bed. Anything that would help her understand what was happening. She didn't know any of the people in the house. It seemed like they just kept coming, that they swarmed in and didn't leave. She searched their faces, hoping to find any of them who might look familiar or give her some comfort. She looked for the big man with dark eyes and a somber expression. Then her father appeared. He was in his pajamas, his hair unkempt. But she realized quickly it wasn't from him being in bed. He dragged his hands back through it, pulling on it as he paced among the strangers.

Her heart felt heavy in her chest when she saw the stretcher come into the entryway. The white sheet over it was just as terrifying as the silence where there should have been sirens. The sheet wasn't to keep someone warm or to protect them. It was so no one could see what was beneath. She was just starting to learn that. There were just enough years to her name for her to start to notice the odd habits and rituals people went through to somehow guard the other people around them, even if it was just for show. Like everyone was walking around surrounded by a thin, fragile, glass shell and you did whatever you could to stop from cracking those shells.

Only this time, she wasn't sure who was being protected. Was it the privacy of the person beneath the sheet? Or was it the emotions of the people around it?

Part of her wished the sheet wasn't there. She already knew who was under it. Though it didn't make sense. Though it was the worst thing she could imagine. If the sheet wasn't there, she would have to see it, and then she wouldn't be able to deny it. This way, there would be a voice in the back of her mind for the rest of her life.

Was it really her?

Could it have been someone else?

At least she wouldn't mind that voice. There was another, a stronger, louder one that forced its way into her thoughts and overtook everything. If the sheet was gone, that voice wouldn't have been there either.

Were her eyes open?

It wouldn't be until years later that she understood why that question stood out to her. Why it bothered her so much to think about. It wasn't that she wanted to know if those warm, reassuring blue eyes she would never see again were open beneath the sheet. It was because it bothered her to think about them being covered that way. She wanted to know if she saw what happened to her.

Someone did this. It wasn't an accident. It wasn't something that just happened because her body gave out. Someone willfully and purposely killed her mother.

But she didn't know who. And she didn't know why.

Mama wasn't even supposed to be there. She should have been gone.

The people she didn't recognize took her father away while she sat there and watched. He didn't come back until later when the house was quiet, and the cold had crept from her toes up her legs and to her fingertips. She didn't know what to say to him. He barely made it into the house. Instead, he shut the door behind him and slid down to the floor, like there was a wall in front of him he couldn't pass through.

She went to sit beside him, then. Just so she could be close to him and not have to feel so alone. There wasn't anything she could do. She knew that. But she was scared.

She scolded herself for it. She was too old to be scared, to want to curl up in his arms and cry. It was only earlier that day she wondered if she was getting too old for the Easter basket she'd hoped to find Sunday morning. Now she told herself she was too old to be afraid, to feel alone, after her mother's murder.

CHAPTER TWELVE

HIM

SEVENTEEN YEARS AGO...

His stomach turned, bile rising up in his throat and burning his lips. The breath locked in his lungs ached against his chest and left his stomach hollow. Thoughts spun through his head, creating a blur of color and pain, questions breaking through and screaming down the back of his neck.

How could this happen? How could they let this happen?

Rage blackened his veins. Acid seared through his body. Horror tore at his intestines, tangling them until he felt like he was strangling from the inside. He couldn't think. He couldn't breathe.

He had been so clear. Every instruction. Every detail was precise. Exact. They knew what they were meant to do. He trusted them.

That was his mistake. He never should have trusted them. He never should have offered a piece of himself up that way. No one deserved that. He had tried to offer it before. There was a time when he willingly reached within himself and took another piece, a hidden piece no one had ever seen, and held it out.

He offered it to her. Was ready to give it over to her without hesitation. It was all he ever wanted. He knew from the first moment he

61

saw her. The first time he drew breath into his lungs in her presence was the first time he breathed. The first time his heart beat in the same space as hers, blood flowed through previously empty veins. That was the day everything changed for him.

But she didn't know then. She'd already been swayed by another. All it took was a first glance, and she was misled. He didn't stop. He didn't lose hope or give up. He knew what she was meant for. What she could be. He offered himself to her, offered her the life she could have. It was a life she never could have imagined. But by then, she was already too deep. He waited just too long, and the other man twisted her mind. Poisoned her heart. She was his, and one day she would understand it.

It wasn't her fault. She couldn't be blamed for the manipulation and deceit of another.

But it had gone too far. He offered her more. He gave fully of himself and ensured she would never truly be without him. But even then, she didn't understand. The other had taken such full control over her mind and her thoughts that she couldn't even see the truth. All he wanted was to take it all away and show her the life and love that was meant for her. He wanted to cradle her in his arms, and guard her from the world, protect her from all that changed her and hurt her.

There was never a moment when he wasn't thinking of her. Even when his hands touched another, he was touching her. When his mouth found soft lips, he was kissing her. When he heard another voice whisper in their sweet mother tongue, it was her words. That woman tried, but she could never give him what he wanted. What was truly his. Just a shallow replica. Now a lingering reminder.

But never enough.

Mariya was everything.

She was meant to be his everything. That night was meant to be the beginning. They were going to rescue her, to save her from what held her and kept her blinded. He would be there to free her and open her eyes. When it was finally done, they wouldn't have to be apart anymore.

And now he had nothing.

Anger reddened the edge of his vision, blurring everything around him. It was like looking down a tight, narrow tunnel, unable to perceive anything else around him. All he could focus on was the screen in front of him. On it was a shaking image of the house taken from a helicopter because the media couldn't get their vans close enough. The narrow road leading to the densely tree-lined, well-hidden drive was blocked off by police cars, an ambulance, and a fire engine. He didn't understand why they sent a fire engine. There was nothing they could do. There was nothing any of them could do.

They sent them anyway. The moment they got the call, they sent out every person they possibly could. As if they thought the uniforms did something or the badges meant something. As if they could make it all go away, reverse time and make it so his heart hadn't been ripped from his chest and his breath hadn't been stopped.

The silent sirens told the truth. They didn't really believe they could do anything for her. Even if they pretended they did. Even if they wanted others to believe they responded to the call with urgency and intention. If they really believed they would be able to do anything for her, the sirens would have cut through the darkness even before the lights did. They were still swirling in their silence. The lights caught attention, but they weren't urgent. They told that something happened rather than that something may. It was an announcement, not a warning.

But it wasn't the lights that mattered. It wasn't even the silence where there should have been sirens or the presence of the fire truck among the ambulance and police officers. It was the flash of a face he saw among the chaos. That one moment, likely not even intended by the photographer, sank into his skin and twisted everything within him. Those weren't the eyes he was supposed to see staring back at him from the aftermath. They were the right tears, the right look of shock and confusion, but the wrong eyes.

That's when he knew what happened. As much as he wanted to be there when it happened, he knew he couldn't. The whole reason he sent the others was to distance himself. Their plan was seamless, but he knew even he could slip through the cracks. It rarely happened. He was meticulous and rarely did something pass by him. But he wasn't immune. He knew that. There was always the possibility of something unexpected happening, and he didn't want to be the one to take the fall. Then all would be lost. There would be no purpose behind any of this.

If anyone was to take responsibility, it would be the men who offered themselves to his service. They would willingly give of their freedom to please him, to protect him.

It meant he had to stay away. He could only wait to hear what happened. They wouldn't come to him. They needed to get as far away from the house as they could. All they could offer him was a simple message. Unassuming, seemingly unrelated. But it told him they had done what they were sent to do. It was his cue to turn on the television in the hotel room at the edge of town. He'd rented out the room several days before and would stay there for a few more to redirect any suspicion.

There had been plans for those days. He'd looked forward to them, had known in his heart they would be filled with the first steps of creating his new life.

He turned on the television and flipped through to the news channel. He wanted the first moments. The reactions and alerts. He wanted to experience everything. Even if he had to be at a distance and couldn't be there the way he wanted to be, he could at least hear the tension and anxiety in the voices of the people reporting. He could enjoy the scurrying emergency responders. If he was extremely lucky, he would get a glimpse of the gurney as they brought out the body.

He wished he could see her face looking back at him from the aftermath. But she wasn't there. She was traveling and would only have just heard what happened. He wouldn't have the chance to see her reaction until he went to her.

But that's when he saw those eyes looking back at him. Among the officers and EMTs. Among the men in suits who arrived so much faster than he ever would have thought they could. He saw eyes he shouldn't have seen.

Then he knew. He knew the mistake that had been made.

He didn't have to hear it from anyone. No one had to confirm it to him. In that instant, everything within him turned to dust.

But he wasn't going to let it destroy him. At least, not all of him. The moment she died, he died along with her. All that was left was the pure, searing hatred of the ones who had caused this, and the need to get his revenge.

CHAPTER THIRTEEN

NOW

The end of January has never been a particularly important milestone for me, but this year it feels different. By the end of January, most people have put away their reminders of the holiday season and are looking ahead to spring. That means I don't think as much about Sarah and the chaos she created in my life. Sam and I are recovering together, piecing our lives back together as much as we can with lingering questions still hovering over us. I wonder if it will ever really not be that way. Will there ever be a time in my life when I don't have questions? When everything has been answered for me and I can just... live?

For now, I'm choosing to take pleasure in the little things that distract my mind from what I don't know and what I'm aching to find out. Today that means Game Night with Janet and Paul across the street. It's less uncomfortable now to go over there, just a fence and an empty plot of land away from the house that became the epicenter of my torment last fall. With those questions answered and the walk through the empty room complete, it's gone back to being just a house.

But even more importantly, Game Night means snacks, and I've been called on to create my signature treat to fuel the four of us through the challenges of Pictionary. The house smells warm and cozy with the richness of butter and cinnamon, and I poke through a cabinet in search of actual sustenance to stop me from eating half the pan of cinnamon rolls before tonight.

"Have I told you recently how beautiful you are and how happy I am to have you in my life?" Sam asks from the table behind me.

I look over my shoulder at him and laugh as I close the cabinet.

"Are you talking to me or to the cinnamon roll?"

"Is it wrong if I say both?" he asks.

"Not at all. I feel pretty happy to have them in my life, too."

Sam gets up and comes over to me. He wraps one arm around me and feeds me a chunk of cinnamon roll with the other hand. It melts on my tongue and makes my belly feel warm.

"And I am extremely happy to have you in my life," he grins. "I don't know if I can ever tell you that enough."

I lick away some of the cinnamon and icing from the corner of my mouth and watch his eyes trace the movement of my tongue.

"Well, I don't mind hearing it. You can say it as much as you'd like."

"I am extremely happy to have you in my life," he whispers again.

He's slowly backing me toward the hallway to the bedroom when the doorbell stops him. He looks at me strangely.

"Are you expecting someone?" he asks.

It's not a possessive or jealous question, but a practical one. Mine isn't exactly the house people just show up at. Everybody I spend any time with is either in Quantico, at work, or standing here kissing me.

"No," I frown.

He leaves me where I'm standing and goes over to the window to peer out at the front porch. A quizzical look on his face, he crosses to the door and opens it. The storm door is locked, another of the habits he's gotten me into when I'm at home. I don't have to brace for someone rushing us, but my curiosity creeps up even higher when I realize Sam isn't talking to anyone. Instead, he unlocks the door, bends down to pick something up, and then leans forward to look up and down the street. He's staring at an envelope in his hand when he comes back into the house and locks the door behind him.

"This is all that's out there," he tells me, holding out the envelope. "I don't know who left it. The mail carrier isn't out there."

"You didn't see anybody?" I ask. He shakes his head.

"It's possible it ended up in the wrong mailbox, and one of the neighbors just swung by and dropped it off."

I take the envelope and look down at it. My breath catches slightly when I read the return address. "It's from Feathered Nest," I tell him.

"What is it?" he asks, stepping closer so he can look at the letter.

I open the envelope and pull out a piece of paper folded once down the middle.

E mma, it's urgent I see you. I'll meet you at the station when you arrive.

I reach back into the envelope and pull out what's left. I hold it up for Sam to see.

"It's a train ticket."

"A train ticket?" he frowns, taking the ticket from me to examine. "Who is the letter from?"

"Marren Purcell. I met her when I was on assignment in Feathered Nest last year," I explain.

"Do you know her well?"

I shake my head, staring down at the letter and trying to process the strange message.

"No. I mean, I spoke to her several times while I was there, but we didn't become close friends or anything. We haven't even kept in touch since I left. To be honest, I haven't even thought about her until right now."

"Then how did she get your address?" he asks.

"I have no idea." I look at the envelope again and point to the upper corner.

I head for what amounts to an office in one of the spare bedrooms, and he comes after me. "Where are you going?"

"I'm calling Marren."

A bank of filing cabinets holds all the papers and folders from my previous cases, and I pull open a drawer. Sam steps up beside me and watches me dig through the contents.

"Leave it to you to actually keep hard copies of everything," he chuckles.

"They're more reliable than computers a lot of times," I point out.

"What are you looking for?"

"The notebook I used when I was in Feathered Nest. If I wrote down her phone number, it would be in there."

"You wouldn't have put it in your phone?" he asks.

"It's possible, but I hope not. That was a burner I only had when I was undercover. I don't have it anymore." I find the notebook and yank it out, sitting down on the oatmeal-colored carpet. "Here it is."

Flipping through the pages of notes makes my head swim. I haven't looked through them since I shoved them out of sight in the filing cabinet. Not that I haven't had to face pieces of them. Scans and copies of many of the pages have shown up in the trial. But actually seeing my handwriting change, the way the words became more erratic and strangely placed across the pages, is an uncomfortable reminder of what I was going through during that time.

Part of me still questions why Creagan chose me for that assignment in the first place. It was my first time going undercover in six months after a slip of judgment and loss of control wrenched me out of the field and sent me to desk duty. I was eager to get back out there, but he tossed me into the deep end with little to buoy me. Looking back, I know I wasn't in the right state of mind to be crawling through the depraved depths of a serial killer's thoughts. Not when it hit so close to home.

"Are you alright?" Sam asks, resting his hand on my back.

I realize I have no idea how long I've been staring at the notes in my hands. I clear my throat and flip the page.

"Fine. It's like looking into someone else's life in a lot of ways, you know? I lost myself so much during that case," I say.

"You didn't lose yourself," Sam replies, lowering down to sit on the carpet, one leg tucked under him and the other bent behind me so I can lean back and rest against his thigh.

"It felt like I did. Everything I knew and believed in. All my training. I let myself get to a place where none of it mattered. Something got under my skin, and all that went right the hell out the window. That investigation was completely messed up in so many ways."

"And yet you brought it to a close. You did what the police in that town weren't able to do. You solved the disappearances and murders, and you brought the perpetrator to justice," Sam points out.

"But I did it based on instinct and emotion. I didn't go through the process or do what the Bureau would have expected of me."

"Listen to me, Emma," he starts, "your instincts are the strongest I have ever known. It's your instincts that allow you to be as incredible at your job as you are. But what you need to remember is you are a human first, an agent second. It might have been Emma the human who solved that case, but it could have been Emma the agent who destroyed it. If you followed every bit of protocol, it might have ended a very different way. Because you didn't hesitate, because you didn't hide behind regulations and expectations, because you didn't shoot first and think later, because you did what you believed you needed to do at every moment, you stayed alive. You were able to follow the trail that brought justice to all those people. Any other choice and they might still be there in that basement. There might be more. You did exactly what you should have done, Emma. Don't second-guess yourself."

I turn over my shoulder and touch a kiss to Sam's lips.

"Thank you," I say softly, resting my forehead against his.

CHAPTER FOURTEEN

"Any luck?"

We've been searching my notebook for nearly an hour with nothing to show for it. Flipping through the rest of the pages, I let out a sigh and shake my head.

"I don't see it. I kept the contact information I gathered close together so I could reference it easily, but it's not on any of those pages. I don't see it on anything else, either."

"Is there a phone book for Feathered Nest? A directory or something that may have her number listed?" Sam asks.

A quick scroll through my phone pulls up the sparse websites for the tiny town.

"This was apparently a passion project for the mayor about ten years ago," I tell him. "He wanted to increase tourism to the area and thought having an internet presence would accomplish that."

"Well, having a serial killer certainly did it for him," Sam points out.

I nod and scan the site. It's mostly a listing of businesses and local events. I point to the screen.

"The Valentine's Day banquet," I say. "One of the victims didn't make it home from that two years ago."

"Did you see this?" Sam asks, pointing higher on the list to events earlier in the year. "Halloween ghost tours of the woods."

"With a stop at Cabin 13. That's not disturbing at all," I comment.

"Directory," Sam says, pointing at a tiny link toward the top of the screen.

Clicking on it brings up a list of the residents of Feathered Nest, conjuring images of their faces as my eyes scan down the names. I don't recognize all of them. It's a small town, but not small enough for me to have come in contact with everyone who lives there in just the few months I lived there. But a good percentage of the names bring up memories. I can see them sitting on the tall stools at Teddy's and roaming among the shops in the village. I see the looks of suspicion and others of kindness.

My time in Feathered Nest is the only undercover assignment that gave me any feelings of guilt. Assuming the identity of another person was a basic part of my job as an agent. I've gone undercover in many different situations, among different people. Being a different person lets me meld into the surroundings and assimilate myself with the people involved in the case so I can bring it to a close. That never means anything more to me than a means to an end. Sinking down into the crime means seeing it from a different angle and dissolving it from the inside. Every time I walk away from those investigations, the only people I carry with me are the victims. How I impacted everyone else I encountered is always far from my mind.

That wasn't the case with Feathered Nest. There was something different about that investigation and the people involved in it from the very beginning. As soon as I arrived at the tiny, isolated cabin tucked in the woods on the outskirts of town, I knew it wasn't going to be like any other case I ever worked. The more I immersed myself among the people in the town, sharing their lives and laughter, the more things blurred between who I was pretending to be and who I actually was.

Creagan had created a backstory for me to explain why I was there. I was looking for a new beginning and considering moving into Feathered Nest. All things considered, it wasn't inaccurate. I really did need a new beginning after having lost my judgment on a previous case. The people of Feathered Nest were lovely. They were kind and friendly, welcoming me, thinking I was going to be one of them. A neighbor. They wanted to bring me into their fold and make me feel comfortable in what might become my home.

When it was all over, and I left town not as Emma Monroe a potential new resident, but as Emma Griffin, FBI agent, I felt like I had betrayed many of them. I did what I was sent there to do. Perhaps not in the way the team would have wanted me to, but I got the job done. I put away a monstrous serial killer who had been terrorizing the town for a long, long time. A man so twisted he manipulated me into a relationship with him so I could be his next victim. He was a perfect young man, handsome and kind and helpful, and everyone in town loved him. But when I showed up, I exposed the shadows underneath.

It wasn't just Jake. I made false connections with people who'd done nothing wrong and yet got swept up in all of it. They were frightened, confused, fearful of what was happening to their tranquil little town, never knowing who to trust. In a way, I both restored their sense of calm and further damaged their ability to trust others. I can't help but think I left Feathered Nest somewhat more closed than when I found it.

Not that it was entirely sunny and welcoming. There were bitter, brutal secrets in that town, and many of the names on this list knew about them. For every person who welcomed me, there were just as many who would just as soon kick me out. They made no secret that I was unwelcome. A stranger meddling where she shouldn't.

"She's not listed," I tell Sam when I get to the bottom of the directory. "I guess I don't really have much of a choice."

I exit out of the browser and bring up my contacts list. Sam looks at me questioningly.

"Who are you calling?"

"Chief LaRoche," I say, not even bothering to try to keep the distaste out of my voice.

"Why are you calling the police chief?" Sam asks.

Before I can say anything to him, the receptionist at the police station answers.

"Chief LaRoche, please," I say.

"Who's speaking?" she asks.

"Emma Griffin."

The beat of silence isn't flattering, but it's not long enough to go all the way to offensive.

"Just a moment," she says.

It takes a few seconds before the phone picks up again.

"Emma Griffin," LaRoche answers. "This is a surprise."

"Hello, Chief. How are things?" I ask.

I hope he doesn't take the question and run with it, but a little bit of common courtesy feels appropriate in the situation.

"Doing well. But I'm assuming that's going to change in the next few moments, considering you are on the phone."

I don't give him the satisfaction of an exasperated sigh.

"All I want is a phone number," I tell him.

"A phone number?" he asks.

"Yes. I need to get in touch with Marren Purcell, but she isn't listed in the directory."

LaRoche is the one who gets to give the sigh.

"I'm not running a phone company here, Griffin. This is a police station. Now, I know your ideas about what police are supposed to do are a little shaky, but I can promise you, helping you chat away on the phone with someone isn't on the list."

"Seriously, LaRoche, I just need to talk to her. I got a letter from her asking me to come back to town, and I want to make sure everything's alright with her," I tell him.

"She wrote you a letter? But you don't have her phone number?" he asks.

"Perhaps you're beginning to see the issue."

"Not particularly, and it's not my place to give out private contact information for one of my citizens. Especially someone who chose not to be included in the town directory. Unless you are on official business. I'm assuming you're not on official business."

"No," I tell him through gritted teeth.

"Well, I do have some things to take care of, so I'll tell Marren you were asking after her next time I see her."

"Can you make that sooner rather than later?" I ask.

"Excuse me?"

"Just go over to her house. Check and make sure she's alright," I sigh, irritated. I'd forgotten how much LaRoche gets on my nerves.

Sam looks at me strangely, and I close my eyes, shaking my head.

"You might not realize this, Griffin, but I actually have a job to do. I'm not just getting kittens out of trees and closing down moonshine stills out here."

"I'm not asking you to spend the afternoon riding a tandem bicycle with her, LaRoche. I just want you to do a welfare check. Tell her I got her letter, and I'm coming. It's not that difficult."

"Goodbye, Miss Griffin." The click on the other end of the line told me he had decided our conversation was over.

"Chief might not have been the best choice," Sam says, getting to his feet and reaching down to help me up.

"He's the Chief of Police, Sam. He's the one who checks on people. What did you want me to do? Give Jake a call?"

"He probably wouldn't be terribly much help either."

I let out a sigh and shake my head. I reach over for the envelope again, turning it over and over in my hands. I stare at it for a long moment, contemplating what in the world is going on. But then I notice something. The odd reality of the letter creeps up the back of my neck, sending stinging pricks along my skin. It isn't just the strange appearance of it and the question of how Marren got my address. It's the name jotted in the opposite corner in tight, slanted writing embedded deep in the envelope.

Marren Purcell. MP. The same initials as Mary Preston.

And Mariya Presnyakov.

CHAPTER FIFTEEN

LAMB

FOUR MONTHS AGO...

Maybe he could have run. That could have been his chance. He knew that's what people would think if they knew what happened. There was no one walking beside him. There were no chains to hold him down; no weapons held to his spine to keep him compliant. He didn't have to follow the path laid out for him. At any second, he could have taken off, escaped through the back, told someone what was happening. He could have deviated from what he was supposed to do and chosen his own way. Saved his own life.

He did. They didn't realize that. They didn't understand the significance of every choice he made when he went inside. The significance of every moment that passed. His steps might not have been far from the path chosen for him, but they carried him further than anyone realized.

He didn't know what was about to happen. He had to keep up the appearance of doing as he was instructed.

Do you understand me, Lamb? Do you know what you are to do?

Walk in. Go to the back. Use the key. Walk out.

Don't call attention to yourself. Don't speak to anyone.

But he did. He spoke just five words. Five words, in case she followed.

"Give this to Emma Griffin."

Those five words were all he could do in that moment. He couldn't run. He couldn't escape. There might not have been anyone beside him, but he wasn't alone. There were eyes on the building, eyes on the doors. They were counting seconds, counting heartbeats. At the designated time, he was supposed to walk back out, straight through the door he entered, and cross the parking lot. They wouldn't speak to him. He wouldn't even know where they were. But they would be waiting.

They could be anyone, anywhere. Lotan didn't tell him who would be watching or give him instructions to check in with anyone when he left. That would have been too easy. It would have given too much away. Instead, he told him what to do and warned him he would know if it wasn't done.

No door was safe. No escape was realistic. At least, he didn't think so then. He carried the heaviness of the lives around him as he walked and drew the key from his pocket. He did everything with a tremendous awareness of every person there. Most didn't even know he was there. They didn't notice him as they scrambled around, handling last-minute details or sank into the boredom of waiting. That was a different kind of waiting. It wasn't the vigilance of the people outside. There was no tension in their waiting. They had no reason to think they didn't know what was coming.

If he didn't walk back through that door when it was expected of him, he would never forgive himself the blood on his hands.

He didn't know the blood would be spilled anyway.

The heat on his back sank through his clothes, and bits of debris blasted through the air cut into his skin. He didn't know what happened. It wasn't until later—when hands grabbed him and dragged him away from the chaos—that he found out.

It wasn't a game. That hit him quickly. For a brief moment, he thought this was just another taunt from Lotan, a reminder of his power. He could dangle him into danger and yank him out just before disaster. He could force him to face the sheer enormity of his influence and cruelty, to make him feel helpless because he didn't know what was going to happen and could do nothing to change it.

"What did you see, Lamb? Who was there?"

"No one. I didn't see anything."

"Nothing?"

"I did what I was told."

"And nothing else?"

"Nothing else."

But not this time. Lotan didn't know what Lamb did. Lamb carried the responsibility of those people for nothing. He offered himself back to Leviathan for no gain. If he had run, they might have shot him. They might have captured him. But maybe not. In the end, the others would face the same fate. He didn't protect anyone.

That one day threw everything off. There was hope, even in the anxiety and bitterness of that day. Those five words. They were his hope. If she heard them, maybe everything would change.

Now he didn't know his next move.

And now he could do nothing but wait for Finn. He didn't know if Finn did everything he was supposed to, but he had to believe he did. That was the only thing keeping him going. It cost a high price for Lamb to get the information he did, and for Finn to share it. Each of those choices, each of those risks, was like a glass capsule of poison. The danger was there but suspended. It could stay harmless, or a single mishap could lead to disaster.

All Lamb cared about now was finding the last piece of the puzzle. He knew so much, but it wasn't enough. Every time he uncovered something else, it only revealed more. But he took those risks, collected the glass capsules. He only needed to figure out one more detail.

Now it was a race.

Who would be found first?

CHAPTER SIXTEEN

NOW

N*ow*
I set the envelope down on the table beside the paper where I wrote the first two names. Sam stares down at them, his eyes slightly narrowed, and his lips twisted like thoughts are churning through his mind.

"I know it's kind of a stretch," I admit. "Her name isn't as close as the others, but it's enough to stand out. Mariya, Mary, and now Marren. The last names are less exact, but they all start with P, and you have to admit the first names are close."

"They are," Sam nods. "It's strange. I'll give you that. What do you know about Marren? You said you didn't really know her very well and didn't spend much time with her. Why would she be reaching out to you now?"

"I don't know. You're right, I didn't spend much time with her, and I don't know her well. I spoke to her a few times, but it wasn't anything deep and meaningful. Just casual conversations. She told me about the town and a little bit about her family. She's a widow and never had any children. The only relative she still had in town was her sister, but she died a few years ago. So, it was just her. I think that's why she wanted to talk to me. Even when other people were starting to get suspicious and not really wanting anything to do with me, she was still willing to have a few words if I wanted to. But, like I said, it didn't amount to much. I honestly don't know why she would want to see me," I tell him.

"Unless it has something to do with the murders," Sam points out.

"Like what? Jake has been in custody for almost a year, and with the exception of having to be relocated, his trial has been seamless." I look down at the papers again. "I just keep coming back to the names. If they do have something to do with each other, Marren writing to me wouldn't have anything to do with the murders from a year ago. But I don't understand what type of link she could have with the bombing or with Mary Preston."

"So, what's that mean?" Sam asks.

"That means I hope I hear from her soon and she has some sort of explanation for why she would reach out to me and how this letter got here."

———

By the time we get back from game night, I still haven't heard anything from Feathered Nest. I can't even enjoy my well-earned victory, but instead go right back into my house and open my computer. Sam sits beside me, chewing on the last of the cinnamon rolls.

"Anything?" he asks.

"Maybe," I offer. "I remembered something while we were playing, and I wanted to check on it. There are a few different types of comments that keep showing up on all of the Mary Preston videos. There are the ones that are about that particular video, the ones that try to create a conversation, and the ones that are more about the person commenting than about Mary. Like this one. This girl, Bella, tries to be the first one to comment on every video." I cringe slightly. "Or I guess, tried. She won't be commenting on any more. But if you look at most of the videos Mary posted, you see Bella is the first one to comment."

I open video after video and point out the comment at the top of each list.

"First," Sam reads, and I nod.

"Yep. That's it. Just 'first'. Apparently, there's some sort of pride in being the first one to comment, even if you're not actually contributing anything to the conversation. She was the first person to comment on every video right up until about eight months ago. Then that switched for a bit."

I pull up the video and show him the first comment. It isn't by Bella, but a profile called SeeAtSea-He-Me. But it's the same message. *First.*

"There's Bella, right after. 'Second'. She's really serious about making herself known," Sam points out.

"Yes, she is. This profile was first for about three videos; then it went back to Bella. I've looked into Bella some. Fairly predictable. Late teens, really enjoys taking pictures of herself. Sometimes her pictures or videos she made seem to correspond with what Mary had done just before that."

"Like she was trying to get Mary's attention with them?" Sam asks.

I shrug. "Maybe, but, again, Mary was trying to make herself into an influencer. Her entire purpose was convincing her followers to think the way she did and try the things she told them to try. Bella was just following along. I've gone through a few of the other videos she liked and commented on. She has a tendency to become attached. Mary seems to be her favorite, but there are a few other people she comments on regularly and subscribes to. That's not unusual for her age range. This is how young people socialize and engage with the world around them."

"You make it sound like we're ancient," he chuckles. "I'm barely in my thirties."

"In some ways, I feel like we're a world away from these kids. It's totally different for them than it was for us. We got together and went to football games or movies. We wandered around town. We hung out in basements. These kids think of people on the other side of the planet as their friends because they can pull up a video of them at any time. It can be a really wonderful thing, don't get me wrong. Being able to reach out to people all around the world is an incredible opportunity. People are able to help each other and learn about each other in a way they never have before. But it also opens up people who are desperate for attention or who want to take advantage of other people."

"Do you think that might be what Mary was doing?" Sam asks.

"I think it's a possibility. She wanted attention. She wanted people to look at her and watch her. Care about what she was saying and what she thought. If you watch the way she speaks and carries herself in her videos, it seems less about truly wanting to teach or introduce things to her viewers, and more like she wanted validation. I have no doubt that she was confident and happy. According to everything I've heard about her, she thought very highly of herself and was determined she was going to make her own way with these videos. But she still had that need for people to admire her and appreciate her. She wanted them to tell her she was beautiful and smart and lucky, to care about what she said."

"These comments definitely look like she was getting what she wanted," he points out.

"Some of them more than others," I nod. "And the ones she responded to the most are the ones that really paid attention to her. Not just the one-off statements of saying she was beautiful or that they loved her outfit. The ones who could pull out specific details or would give a recommendation with a sly compliment she would appreciate because of her taste or that they heard it was fabulous, so she should try it. Almost like they weren't worthy of it, but she was. Those are the ones she picked up on. So, what were they getting out of it? Feeling like they were friends? Feeling special because she responded directly to them? Or something else?" I ask.

"What else do you think it could be?"

"At first, I was intrigued by Bella simply because she kept showing up, but then I realized her interactions with Mary were pretty superficial, and nothing stood out about her profile. Whoever accessed Mary's cloud to send that clip to me was more intense than that. They wouldn't just have a casual connection. So, that's what made me think of this." I point to the 'first' comment by the other profile. "This person is making a point. It's not just about being the first one to comment. It's about being before Bella. The fun thing about the internet is you never know who people actually are. It can be anybody behind a name. Bella could be a spectacular catfish, but I doubt it. She seems pretty transparent. This one, though. SeeatSea-He-Me. There are some question marks."

"Starting with the name," Sam comments.

I click on the name to bring up the user's profile. The avatar is a closeup of a very blue eye, and there is no actual name listed.

"It's unusual. But some people try to get poetic with their profiles. They don't really want it to be about them; it's about their perspective. Sometimes their art. Look, there are dozens of pictures of the ocean. Sunrise, sunset, close to the waves, far away from the waves. These look like she's in the water, like on a boat."

"See at Sea," Sam says, nodding. "Alright. She has a thing for oceans."

"There aren't any clear images of people in any of the pictures. But there are a few that have shadows. These look like a tall guy with broad shoulders. He and me?" I suggest.

"Sure, that makes sense."

"It does, but it doesn't. This profile isn't like most of the other ones leaving comments and following Mary's vlog. It's not about the person. It doesn't fit the pattern of the other consistent followers, but for almost a year, it's been a consistent follower of Mary's videos. Almost three months of just likes. Then the 'first' message. I read through all the comments left from this profile to Mary. They start simple and casual. Then gradually, they become more and more familiar, and Mary spends more time talking back. There are even two instances on the other profile where Mary liked her pictures," I tell him.

"So, what is it you remembered?" he asks.

I select a specific video and open it, scrolling down through the comments.

"This," I say. "This video is from about two weeks before the bombing. Mary is comparing all the different fall flavored coffees that just hit the stores."

"Autumn creep is real. Pretty soon, they are going to have pumpkin spice conversation hearts on Valentine's Day," Sam mutters.

"From your lips to God's ears," I grin. I point out an exchange. "Here they get into a conversation talking about their favorite ways to have flavored coffee. It's fairly mind-numbing, which is why I didn't fully catch it the first time. Right here, SeeatSea says 'those caramel cookies I told you about.'"

"You think that's a code for something?" Sam asks.

"I mean, it could be. Or they could just be, you know, cookies. But let's find out."

I go through every video with comments from SeeatSea and scan for any mention of cookies. When I get to the end, I nod. "Exactly what I thought. She never mentions cookies. Not on any of the videos. Which means they must have been communicating outside of the comments."

I reach for my phone and start dialing.

"Calling LaRoche again?"

"No. Eric. I want to see if he can find out what Mary and SeeatSea were talking about just a few days before she died."

CHAPTER SEVENTEEN

I know Sam well enough by now I can almost tell what he's feeling and thinking without even having to look at him. Just by the way his eyes feel on my back or how his energy surrounds me when he comes into the room, I can come up with a fairly accurate estimation of what's going through his mind. Two days after our deep dive into Mary Preston's comments, when he arrives to bring me to dinner and finds me with my suitcase spread out across my bed, I sense it's not a great reaction. His eyes burrow into the top of my head as I lean over to tuck a rolled pair of socks in the corner of the case. I can feel his hesitation.

"What are you doing?" he asks.

I look up at him and cross to my dresser for more clothes.

"Packing. My train to Feathered Nest is tomorrow."

"You're going?"

He comes into the room and peers down into my suitcase like he can evaluate my state of mind by what I've chosen to put inside. So far, it's socks, underwear, and pajamas, so there's not a lot to go on yet.

"Of course I am. I thought you knew that."

"And I thought you were going to Florida to look more into what Bellamy found," he tells me.

"Not until after I'm able to talk to Christine. I'd really prefer not to go into that situation completely flailing blind. The more she can tell me about her father and the time around my mother's death, the better I'll be able to navigate. For now, this is what I need to do. For one reason or another, Marren needs me. LaRoche finally called back and said he went by her house. She's fine. He didn't tell me anything else, but that might be because she can't trust anyone."

"Except for you?" he raises an eyebrow.

I toss a handful of jeans into the bag and turn a glare toward him.

"Is there some hidden meaning to that comment you want to expand on?" I ask.

"Why would she choose you? You haven't been back there since the investigation ended. What could you help her with?"

"I don't know. But I'm not just going to ignore her because I don't know what she needs. There's a reason I got that letter and the train ticket."

He watches me take another handful of clothes out of the next drawer and add them to the suitcase.

"A letter that showed up on your porch from someone you barely know, and a train ticket when you could just as easily drive to Feathered Nest. Doesn't that seem at all suspicious to you?" he asks, walking up to the side of the bed.

"Of course it does, Sam. But that's why I have to go. Don't you understand that? The darkness in Feathered Nest didn't go away when Jake was arrested. That town is steeped in it, and it just keeps coming to the surface. There are answers in Feathered Nest that I need. I'm not going to ignore this chance to find them."

I go to my nightstand and take out my holster and a box of bullets. Taking my hard-sided case out from under my bed, I dismantle the gun and tuck it inside.

"What are you doing?" Sam frowns.

"I can't have my gun on the train. It has to be dismantled and checked," I explain. "Unless there's official law enforcement activity going on, no one is allowed to have a gun on board. Permit or not. That applies to police and FBI agents, too. Since I'm not on official duty on this trip, it stays in my suitcase until I get to Feathered Nest."

"How about a knife?" he asks.

"Not even allowed in my checked luggage. The best I can do is a pair of scissors or nail clippers."

"I'm serious, Emma," he says. "You have to have something to protect you."

"So am I. Those are the rules. I'm not guarding anyone, and I'm not on official law enforcement business. This is the way it is. At least it will be in the luggage so I can get to it when I get there," I reply.

"Why don't you drive? If you get there and Marren really needs you, then you're there," he suggests. "If there's something else going on, then you didn't get on the train."

"I can't do that, Sam," I tell him.

"Why not? What if you're being lured onto the train?"

"That's exactly why I have to do it."

"Why?" he insists. "Emma, I'm just worried about your safety."

"I can take care of myself, Sam."

"Emma, you've almost been killed several times in the last few months. I can't just—"

"That's not fair," I cut him off. "You know that's not fair!"

"It's true," he fires back. "And here you go again, just leaping into danger without knowing anything about it!"

"I'm a federal agent, Sam. It's not exactly a safe job. And I signed up for this. Same as you when you put on that badge. You can't just keep me back here forever. I'm going to Feathered Nest."

"Emma, why is this such a big deal to you?"

"Because it will never stop, Sam!" I shout.

He's taken aback. I hold up a finger to stop him from talking, then draw out a breath and let it out slowly.

"I still don't know who Ron Murdock was. He died at my feet, and I don't know his real name, why he was there, or how he died. That's not something I can just ignore. He knew my parents, and he came to me for a reason. The necklaces. My father's birth certificate. The video clip. It's never going to stop if I just pretend it's not happening. I can't run from it. It stops when I stop it."

I slam the gun case closed in frustration, trying not to let the emotion tightening my throat seep into my voice. I appreciate him worrying and wanting to protect me. At the same time, the pressure reminds me of exactly why I made the hard choice I did seven years ago. It wasn't easy to walk away from him, to leave him behind and force myself to move ahead into a life where he, and Sherwood, didn't exist. But it's what I had to do to pursue my career. It wasn't just for me. It was for my mother and father, and the questions they left behind. I couldn't have a life that anyone else depended on, or that required me to depend on anybody else. I had to live just for myself, so I could do what needed to be done.

In a lot of ways, it hasn't changed. I can't hold myself back or not follow my instincts because Sam doesn't want me to. This is what I would do, whether I had come back to Sherwood or not. I know he worries about me, but that can't stop me.

I'm tired of the questions. Of not knowing. There's too much of my past hidden in shadow. I need to shine a light on it. I have unfinished business in Feathered Nest. Maybe this will finally let me put the town and its secrets behind me.

CHAPTER EIGHTEEN

"What can I do?" Sam asks with a resigned sigh.

I look up at him suspiciously. "What do you mean?"

"I'm... not going to let you do this by yourself. I understand it's something you have to do. And I know I can't stop you. I might not see what you see, but if you believe you need to follow this, then you need to. What can I do to help you?" he asks.

I pause, searching his face, making sure he's serious. When he doesn't hesitate, I step closer to him.

"The train goes to the station outside Feathered Nest twice every morning. The ticket I got in the mail is for the second run. But what if I was already gone by the time that train ran?"

"And someone is there in your place?" Sam asks.

"Exactly. If I switch my ticket to the earlier train and get you one for the original run, I can look over the train station and make sure everything looks as expected. Then an hour after I leave, you board your train, the original train I was supposed to be on. If this is nothing but Marren actually writing to me and wanting me to come to Feathered Nest, then it'll be a boring few hours, and I'll wait at the station on the other side until she comes to pick me up. But if it's something else, whoever is doing it hopefully won't follow through without me on the train. You keep your eye out for anyone looking suspicious and let me know. I'll be waiting at the other station and can call in security if needed." I draw in a breath. "Only..."

"Only, what?" he asks.

"What if I'm wrong? What if it doesn't matter if I'm on that train or not? I could be tossing you into the lions' den."

"It's worth the risk," he points out. "If someone is trying to get their hands on you, they're going to be precise about it. If you're being lured onto this train, it's for a specific reason. They'll want to see you. They'll want to make sure whatever they have in mind happens."

"I don't want to put you in danger," I tell him. "Not for me."

He smiles. "Now, who's the one worrying too much?"

Despite myself, I smile back sadly, keeping the tears away from my eyes as best as I can. I let out a sound somewhere between a laugh and a sigh and a sob.

"So you're in?"

Sam takes my hand.

"You're right, Emma. It's dangerous, but we signed up for this risk. I can handle myself, and I know you can handle yourself. And besides, this isn't just about you. This could be a threat toward everybody on that train. But it's a threat we can stop, and that's worth the risk."

The next morning Sam arrives so we can have breakfast together. I hand him his coffee as he tells me about calling the train station.

"Getting a ticket on the train wasn't a problem, but they weren't interested in adding any extra security. Since I wasn't able to explain to them any actual threat toward either of us, they aren't willing to do anything. I asked about emergency dispensation for carrying our weapons on board, even me as an officer, but they wouldn't give it to me. No investigation, no case, no gun," he tells me.

"It's alright. I didn't expect to have it, so it doesn't change anything."

Not wanting to call attention to me getting on the train early or to Sam going at all, I drive myself to the train station in Castleville. He will follow soon. Just like I expect, the station is very quiet this early in the morning. I already bought my new ticket online, so I walk inside and scan my surroundings. I pay attention to every person I see waiting on the benches and standing near the doors. I didn't want to have too much time of lingering around in the station and possibly being noticed, so I timed my arrival to give me just enough time to look over the station and check my suitcase before boarding.

The woman behind the desk hands me a claim ticket for my bag, and I tuck it away in the backpack I'm bringing on board before walking around the station, scanning it for anything that strikes me as strange. Nothing seems out of the ordinary, so I walk out onto the platform.

The train is already there. Long and silver. It glistens in the sunlight. Uniformed conductors walk up and down, doing their customary checks as the passengers who traveled from other places disembark. A stream of people head into the station or scurry to the other platform to wait for their connecting train. I stand to the side, watching them as they pass. I hesitate there even when the stream is over, letting the people heading to the platform go by before I make my move.

A few passengers walk past me. I scan each of them, taking note of their luggage and how they interact with everything around them. People are often suspicious without realizing it. The way they carry themselves, how they look at the people around them. They think they're being casual and acting normally, but they're calling attention to themselves. I watch a man set his luggage down at his feet and walk a few feet away to put out a cigarette. Another clutches his messenger bag close to his chest, gripping the strap as he talks rapidly into the phone pressed to his ear. A woman walks with a young child along the platform, fussing over him as if she's torn between wanting him to walk independently and being too impatient to handle his tiny, uncertain steps.

I watch every person who bustles near the entrances, until a conductor appears at one of the narrow doors, gripping the handle and leaning out like he's in a movie.

"Now boarding," he calls. "First class, please go to gate J. All others, come to this door."

I linger back, watching how the passengers disperse. The woman rushes directly to the conductor, her child held tightly in her hand, while the man already sucking on another cigarette puts it out and starts toward the first-class gate. I wait until everyone who has already filtered out of the station boards before getting on. The conductor directs me to the right, and I walk into a nearly empty car. A few of the passengers look at me as I make my way slowly down the aisle, but most are too absorbed in their phones or digging through their bags, taking inventory of everything they forgot when packing.

The man with the messenger bag sits in a window seat with his bag taking up the seat beside him. He's not talking into his phone anymore, but it's gripped tightly in his lap as he stares through the window at the woods beyond the station.

I take a row close to the back of the car, going through the process I learned the last time I traveled by train to Feathered Nest. That was a much longer journey than this one will be. In an effort to conceal my travel path and establish more of a backstory for my undercover persona, I bounced from train to train, weaving and backtracking before finally getting to my destination. It was annoying as hell, but it gave me plenty of time to get my train travel down to a science. Which includes popping up the leg rest from under my seat and pulling out the foot prop from the seat in front of me. The blue fleece blanket rolled up in my backpack is a throwback to one of those train rides, when the chill was so intense it had me shivering until I finally broke down and bought the blanket from the snack car.

Slinging the blanket over my lap now gives me a head start. Next comes lowering the tray and setting up my computer. It'll give me something to do during the next few hours of travel, but for now, it's a prop. Having the computer open in front of me gives me the appearance of doing something, so people don't notice my eyes constantly sweeping across the inside of the car. I take in every person around me. Every movement. I watch out the window at every engineer and bellhop who passes by.

Around me, the train car settles. For several minutes no one else gets on board. It seems the handful of other passengers scattered through the seats are going to be my only companions for the trip. I glance at the time in the bottom corner of my computer screen. We should be moving by now.

Five minutes later, we're still sitting in place. A conductor starts up the aisle, performing the ticket checks usually reserved for the first few minutes after the train starts moving. His gait shifts back and forth as he goes like his body doesn't realize the train is still, like it's so used to his routine it doesn't matter if there's any particular force causing the movement, it's going to happen. He holds a pad of vibrant green sticky notes in one palm and a black marker in the other hand. As he looks at the tickets the passengers show him, he slashes a mark across the sticky note and slaps it into place above the passenger's head.

The marks denote where that passenger is going, so when we reach different stops, he can keep track.

Glance. Slash. Stick. Glance. Slash. Stick.

He gets through the passengers and makes it to my row. One man chose the aisle seat directly across from me, and he sits as far back as he can, already reading a book.

"Mr. Jones," the conductor says, adding the man's bright green header before even looking at his ticket. "Good to see you again."

The man nods. "Good morning, Thomas."

My eyes slide up to the note above his head as the conductor makes his way to mine. I watch Mr. Jones stand up and set his book in his seat before heading down the aisle in the direction of the snack car. He's on his way to Georgia. I glance at the conductor.

"When are we going to leave?" I ask.

"The train has been delayed, but we should be moving shortly," he reassures me.

"What's the delay?"

"I don't know."

He disappears through the doors blocking the walkway between this car and the next. My phone ringing takes my attention, and I fish it out of my pocket.

"Is that your train still sitting at the platform?" Sam asks when I answer.

"Yes. We've been delayed, but the conductor doesn't know why. Are you at the station?"

"Just got here. Give me a second." Muffled sounds accompany footsteps as he carries the phone with him across the station. He asks about the delay, but I can't understand the response. More muffled sounds carry me back to where Sam started. "Apparently there was an issue with a passenger getting off to smoke a cigarette, but not bringing his ticket or ID with him. They already closed the doors when he tried to get back on."

"Is he in first class?" I ask.

"A sleeper car, yeah," Sam says.

"I saw him before getting on the train. That shouldn't be too difficult to figure out. I'm sure we'll be leaving soon."

"Alright. I'll check in with you later."

Tucking my phone away, I wake the screen of my computer back up and see the familiar video paused on a still of Mary grinning down at a massive vanilla milkshake. I press the down arrow on my keyboard until I get to the comments section.

SeeatSea-He-Me: First

CHAPTER NINETEEN

The train finally starts moving twenty minutes later, and as
soon as the announcement says the snack car is open, I'm
ready for coffee. I stuff my computer back in its bag and
under the seat in front of me and go head up the aisle. As I go, I take
note of the people and their green notes. Only two other people in the
car are headed for the station near Feathered Nest, though I doubt
either will end up in the middle of the woods with me. They will more
than likely head to one of the other towns nearby or switch trains and
journey on somewhere else.

Coffee from a snack car in a train is never a gourmet experience,
but a sleepless night and early morning make the little paper cup
gripped in my hand glorious. I'm tempted to just lean against a wall,
down this cup, and get another to bring back to my seat with me.
Instead, I check to make sure the car will remain open for at least the
next couple of hours so I can come back for a refill, then make my
way back to my car. Passing through the two cars that separate the
snack car from mine gives me the opportunity to scan more faces,
check more behaviors. These cars are even more sparsely occupied
than the one I'm in, with the one closest to the snack car only having
three people in it.

My phone ringing in my pocket startles a woman sleeping against the window, and I mouth an apology as I answer.

"Hey, Eric."

"Are you already on the train?" he asks.

I got in touch with both him and Bellamy last night to let them know what was happening. Knowing they know about the plan is like having a safety net under me. I hope I won't need to use it, but it's good that it's there just in case.

"Yes. We got moving a little bit ago."

"How about Sam's train?"

"I haven't heard from him yet. There's still a little bit before it's supposed to leave, but we were delayed, so I don't know if he will be, too," I tell him. "There are so few people on this train. I would think the conductors would want to get everybody into one car. Wouldn't that make it easier to keep an eye on people?"

"They do limit the cars that are available. Some of the ones on that train are probably totally empty. They also anticipate how many passengers are supposed to be boarding at different stations and how long they'll be riding. They let them spread out, so there is no big crush of people moving in and out of a specific area of the train. People also just like to have at least the illusion of choosing their own seats. It gives them a sense of freedom and autonomy, which is one of the most effective means of crowd control," Eric explains.

"Because people who feel like they're being controlled or limited in what they are allowed to do are more likely to push back against it," I say.

"Exactly. Especially when there's the issue of perceived value, like when it comes to train seats."

"What do you mean?"

"Every person assigns importance to different things. That becomes perceived value. You like window seats near the back of the car. Other people prefer aisle seats. Some may really hate the idea of sitting near a bathroom, while others would specifically seek that out. Some want to be in the middle of the car away from the doors, so there isn't as much shuffling around when passengers get on and off.

Other people would rather be close to the door, so they can get off first. It's all about what the individual values. When people are given the freedom to choose their own seats—even if it's limited just by the number of cars available—they feel like they are getting value for what they paid. Assigned seating creates a sense of animosity because inevitably people don't get what is of greatest value to them and will feel slighted," Eric explains.

"I can see where that would bother the guy sitting across from me," I say. "Tons of empty seats and he chooses the one directly across the aisle from me."

"That's a little odd," Eric says.

"Yeah, but I have the feeling it's where he always sits. He and the conductor greeted each other by name. What's strange is he's going all the way to Georgia. That can't be a trip he takes by train every couple of days." I walk back into my car and get to my aisle. His seat is still empty. "And he's still not here."

I thought I muttered it, but it was loud enough for Eric to hear.

"Not there?" he asks.

"He got up while we were still delayed and hasn't come back yet. All his stuff is still here, but he's not."

"Maybe he went to the observation car," Eric offers.

I make a face at the phone even though he can't see me.

"It's a passenger train through small-town Virginia, Eric. There is no observation car."

I turn to my seat and pause. Eric says something, but the words go past me without sinking in.

"Emma?" he says a second later, my name cutting through to get my attention.

"Yeah. I'm sorry. What did you say?" I ask.

"I wanted to let you know I'm still working on getting the transcripts from Mary Preston's vlog. Apparently, they were never requested because there was no reason to believe they had any connection to the bombing."

"Okay. Thanks for doing that for me. Just let me know if you get your hands on it," I say, still staring at my seat.

"Sure. Is everything alright? Your voice changed," he says.

"I'm good. Will you ask Bellamy to look at the profile? She might have some insights."

"Alright," he says, and I finish the call before stepping into my row of seats.

I set my coffee and my phone on the tray table, take my seat, resting my hand on the closed lid of my computer. I reach under the seat in front of me and find my backpack tucked exactly where I put it. Only I know my computer was in it when I put it there. Standing, I look around to see if anyone is paying attention. Eyes slitted to the side toward me, or sudden extreme devotion to a menial task might give away who took it out. But the passengers ahead of me seem oblivious to the world around them. The young mother is reading to the little boy curled up with his head in her lap. Two of the others are reading. A few more are sleeping or plugged into earbuds, lost in whatever is playing on the devices in their laps.

I'm sitting again when my peripheral vision catches someone sitting two rows behind me. He wasn't there before. No one was sitting behind me when I left to get my coffee. I walk out into the aisle and briefly lift my eyes to check for a green note above his head. It's there, announcing his journey to Florida, the last stop on this route.

"Did you see someone near this seat?" I ask, pointing toward my seat.

The man looks up from the sketchbook he has propped on the tray table in front of him. He glances in the direction I'm pointing, then looks at me and shakes his head. Dark hair cut close to his head and intense blue eyes give him a distinctive appearance that doesn't seem to fit with the pencil sketch on the paper in front of him.

"No."

"No one?" I frown. "You didn't see anyone near this seat?"

He shakes his head again, then eyes me carefully.

"Were you wearing a sweater?" he asks.

"A sweater? No, I was not wearing a sweater," I tell him, the sharp 't' sounds dipped in more acid than may have been necessary.

"Then, yes," he nods, straightening up and pointing at me with the eraser of the pencil in his hand. "When I came back from the restroom, there was a woman in that row. I leaned down to get my pad out, and when I looked back, she was walking out of the car. She had on a blue sweater, and her hair was pulled up like yours. I didn't get much of a look at her, so I just assumed it was you."

I didn't see anyone who looked like that in the cars I walked through on the way back from the snack car, so I point to the door behind him.

"She left in that direction?" I ask. He nods. "You weren't here when I left."

"What?"

"You weren't sitting here. When I left to get coffee, there was no one sitting back here."

"You might not have seen me, but I was here." He gestures up toward the green note. "Conductor-approved."

I walk back to my seat and lift the computer screen. My fingers tremble as I peel away a bright green sticky note adhered inside.

CHAPTER TWENTY

The door to the car opens, and the conductor starts down the aisle again. He's not checking tickets this time, just glancing at the sticky notes and the people sitting beneath them. I wonder how many times he does this a day, and how often he barely even notices what he's seeing. Everything is so routine, so consistent it must just flow through his brain and barely register unless there's something seriously wrong. That seems to happen when he gets to the aisle between my seat and the one beside me. I tuck the note I found in my computer out of sight and watch him stare down at the empty seat.

"He hasn't come back since the train started," I mention.

The conductor looks over at me, seemingly confused to have heard my voice.

"Excuse me?" he asks.

"The man who is sitting in that seat. You called him Mr. Jones? He got up while the train was still delayed at the station, and he hasn't been back. He didn't bring anything with him, so I don't think he moved seats."

"Thank you," he nods.

That's it. With no other response, he continues past me and the man drawing in the sketch pad to go into the next car. I take out the note again and look at it. The black ink across the vibrant green is difficult to decipher, but it looks like the initials for the Castleville station, where I boarded. Running my finger across the mousepad, I wake up the screen. Nothing seems changed. The same video is up that was when I closed it. There are no new windows or anything moved. It's as if the woman took the computer out just so she could put the sticker inside and walk away.

I stuff my computer back into my bag and sling it over my shoulder as I shuffle into the aisle and head in the same direction the conductor went, the direction the other passenger said the woman walked after leaving my seat. A button opens the sliding door, and I step into the small vestibule. Metal plates beneath my feet shift and bounce at the coupling, a stark reminder I'm briefly between two cars rather than actually in one.

The next door opens for me, and I start down that aisle, glancing at each passenger as I go. Though I'm looking for a sweater the way the man described, I'm aware the woman might have very well taken it off, so I keep my eye out for someone blonde. I get to the end of the car with no one matching the description and pass through another connector into the next car. The conductor is still in this one, making his way along the rows and checking on passengers. There is only one blonde woman in this car, and she is considerably shorter than me, with a glossy bob. He couldn't have mistaken me for her even with only a partial glance.

I'm making my way toward the end, expecting the conductor to just continue through, but he stops and turns back around. His eyes narrow when he sees me.

"Can I do something for you?" he asks in a lowered tone, coming closer like he doesn't want me to disturb the passengers.

"Oh, no. Thank you. I'm just looking for someone," I tell him.

"Mr. Jones?" he asks suspiciously.

"No," I reply. "Someone else. She stopped by my seat when I was in the snack car. I apparently just missed her. She's not in this car, though, so I'm just going to check in the next."

I start to move around him, but he shifts into my path.

"You will not find her in the next car," he says simply.

"How do you know that? I didn't even describe her."

"I know that because the next three passenger cars are empty. Beyond that are the first-class sleep accommodations," he tells me.

"The cars are empty?" I ask.

"Yes. The last of those passengers disembarked. There won't be further passengers in those cars until we reach the end of this leg."

Meaning they won't pick anyone else up until we get to the station outside of Feathered Nest.

"So, you won't go into those cars until we get to the station?" I ask.

"No. My responsibility is to the passengers, and since there are none in there, and those in this car have been instructed the doors between the cars are locked, there's no point in going in there," he says.

"You don't think it's worth going in there even though you have a missing passenger?" I ask.

Thomas draws in a breath, squaring his shoulders as he plasters on a fake smile and gestures for me to back up, so I'm away from the others in the car.

"We don't have a missing passenger," he says in a lowered tone as he continues to guide me up the aisle. "Simply because Mr. Jones is not sitting in his seat right now doesn't mean he's missing. I'll thank you not to disrupt the other passengers. Inciting panic is taken very seriously."

"I'm not trying to incite panic," I tell him. "I just..."

"Good. Then, please return to your seat. I'm sure your friend will come back to your seat when she has a chance."

He continues walking directly behind me until I've gone through the next connector. I make my way back to my seat and drop my bag into the seat beside me before sitting down and taking out my phone.

Sam answers on the first ring.

"We got started right on schedule," he tells me. "So, we're not too far behind you. Everything is calm so far. Nothing weird or unusual. I don't get a strange vibe from anyone I've seen so far."

"It's not as calm here," I say, keeping my voice low so my words don't drift out into the aisle, to be heard by other passengers.

"What do you mean?" Sam asks, sounding tense. "What's going on?"

"I'm not sure yet. Maybe nothing. When I went to get coffee from the snack car, I put my computer in my bag, under the seat in front of me. But when I came back, it was sitting on my tray table, closed. I opened it and there was a sticky note inside."

"A sticky note?" Sam asks.

"Has the conductor come by to check your ticket?" I ask.

"Yes."

"The note he put above your head to say where you're going. In this car, they are bright green sticky notes. There was one on the inside of my computer, stuck to the screen. The destination on it was Castleville. Nobody in the car seemed to be paying any attention to what was going on, but there's a guy sitting a few seats behind me who said he saw a blonde woman near my seat. She apparently walked away not too long before I came back," I explain. "So, it's entirely possible some woman has been on the train for hours, is bored, and was wandering around trying to find something to entertain herself. She found the sticky note on the floor from one of the passengers who had just got off and left it in my computer as some weird joke."

"I mean, that's certainly an explanation," Sam acknowledges. "But how would she know there was even a computer in your bag? I'm aware you can drink your volume in hot beverages, but I can't imagine you spent so much time in the snack car some woman could come poke around in your bags without someone thinking she looked suspicious."

"And where is she now?" I ask.

"What do you mean?"

"I went through the next two passenger cars looking for her since the guy who saw her said that's the direction she left. But I didn't see anyone who looked even remotely like what he described, and the conductor told me the other passenger cars are empty. They are the ones for the passengers who got off before I boarded in Castleville.

Which makes two missing passengers. The man sitting across the aisle from me got up during the delay, and I haven't seen him since."

"Did you tell the conductor?" Sam asks.

"I did. He didn't seem concerned and actually scolded me for suggesting he was missing. Which I found strange. He knows this guy by name. He knows where he sits," I say.

"Then maybe he knows of strange habits he has. Keep your eyes open. If anything else happens, let me know."

"I will."

As I pull my computer out again, the bag slips from the seat onto the floor. I lean over to pick it up and glance toward the back of the car, where I find the sketch artist's intense blue eyes staring at me. They quickly flicker away, but they don't take their strange chill with them.

CHAPTER TWENTY-ONE

I've been on the train for just over two hours when an announcement comes through the car telling passengers the snack car would be closing for a lunch break. As soon as I hear that, I close my computer and put it away. The intense blue eyes follow me as I make my way through the sliding door. Lunch break for the snack car often means the conductors are taking a break as well. That gives me a short time to move through the cars without Thomas being there to sweep me back to my seat.

The sticky note pressed to my palm, I move through the first car and then the second. My eyes follow the curves of every face in every seat, ensuring I remember them, seeing if anyone new has appeared, but they are all the same. No one is paying attention when I get to the end of the second car. The lull of the train keeps them from noticing I haven't turned back around. Instead, I walk up to the door Thomas mentioned is locked. I press the button, and the door slides open.

I dip through as quickly as I can, satisfied by uncovering the lie, but not wanting to be noticed. The empty car is eerie in its silence. Rows of seats look strangely abandoned in the dark car, though I know they were occupied only hours before. Now that I'm inside, my steps slow, and I follow the aisle gradually. I don't know exactly what

I'm looking for, but I hope to find it. There are no notes tucked into the spaces above the seats. Overhead compartments stand open, ready for the luggage of passenger's hours in the future. There isn't even an errant candy wrapper on the navy blue carpet.

At the end of the car, there's another sliding door. The only light coming through the window is sunlight, casting shadows into the next car. I press the button, not expecting it to open. It doesn't, so I search it for a mechanism I can release. Eventually, I tuck my fingers into the gap between the door and the frame and apply pressure, forcing it apart. If there's one thing I've learned about safety mechanisms in public places, it's that safety comes before security. The doors might technically lock to stop passengers going into certain cars, but they don't seal or clamp in place. Though rare, train crashes do happen, and it's critical passengers be able to get out of the cars, even if they have to pry the doors open.

The second door requires a bit more convincing, but finally, it opens, and I walk into the next empty car. Halfway down the aisle, I notice something different from the first passenger-less car. Tucked into the mesh pouch on the back of a seat is a pair of earbuds. The black wire is barely noticeable, but when I look at it closer, I notice it's not just the buds hanging from their cord in the mesh. Instead, they are looped over a magazine and attached to a tablet partially hidden out of view.

I'm tempted to touch it, to pull it out and examine it, but I stop myself. Instead, I use my phone to snap a picture of it. The sticky note feeling hot on my palm, I leave the seat and continue to the end of the car. The window is dark and shadowy like the last.

It feels like I'm in a continuous loop, with each train car leading me to one that brings me back to the first. Through the window on the top half of the door, I see another darkened car. More abandoned seats. Overhead compartments mostly open. Not even bothering to try the button, I push my fingers into the gap and tug on the door.

It resists. More than it should. I gather my breath and spread my legs to brace the sides of my feet against the walls on either side of me. I pull harder, but the door still won't move. It feels heavy, straining against my movements. I change positions, turning to push my back against the wall so I can put my hands in the gap and shove forward. Finally, the door gives way and shifts out of place. Only this time, it doesn't move smoothly and easily open.

The body leaning against it stops it partway.

I stumble back, catching a stunned gasp in my throat, as the body slides away from the door and topples backward into the aisle in front of me. It's a man, and as I get closer, I see his throat has been slit.

A dark veil of blood runs down the front of his neck and soaks into his T-shirt. There's little question as to what caused the injury. The hilt of a knife embedded in his stomach sends more blood cascading down his body to pool under him, and pins something to his darkened shirt.

The position of the body at the end of the aisle, sprawled on the carpet in between two walls, means the sunlight coming through the windows isn't enough to fully illuminate him. I use my phone to shine light down on him.

This isn't Mr. Jones. I'd expected the uncomfortable-looking man from across the aisle, but instead, it's a younger, heavier man with a blond beard speckled with blood. The light hits the knife and the object it's holding in place. It's a note, the bold black handwriting large enough to read without picking it up.

You should have gotten on your train, Emma.

My stomach turns. I lift my head to take a breath. I force the bile in my throat back down and try to keep my breathing under control as I take slow steps away from the body. As I do, my phone flashlight sweeps up just enough for me to notice congealed blood drips down the wall in front of me. I follow the trail to reveal words in rough black marker scrawled across the bottom of the door leading into the last of the empty passenger cars.

Want to watch a movie?

My blood turns to ice, and my heart hammers out of my chest. The simplicity and disconnection of the note is chilling. Sickening. I read it again and again, trying to figure out if I'm missing something. I look at the letters, how they're formed. Wondering if there is something else.

Suddenly a thought flashes into my head. I rush back up the aisle to the seat with the earbuds and the magazine. Carefully moving the magazine aside, I pull out the tablet. The screen is black, the battery long worn down, but I flip it over and find a note taped to the back.

Your train. Your responsibility.
Time to play a game, Emma.
Hide-and-seek. Find one before I hide another.
Are you good at keeping secrets?
Is Sam?
You better be.
Time is ticking. If it runs out, if either train stops, if the police come
You blow it.
Catch me if you can.

I dial Sam, fighting to control my breathing so he'll be able to understand me.

"Hello?"

"He's here," I whisper frantically, my words rattling.

"What? What are you talking about?" he asks.

"He's here. At least, he was. I need—I need you to get away from other people so I can video call you."

The few seconds of muffled sounds seem to stretch on endlessly before he finally stops.

"Alright. I'm not near anyone. What's going on?" he asks.

"I'm switching to video."

I hit the button and wait while the screen shifts into an image of Sam. He's standing in the train bathroom with confusion and worry etched on his face, the lights looking impossibly bright and artificial behind him. I walk back to the sliding door and turn the camera toward the body on the floor.

"Oh my God," Sam gasps.

Turning the camera back to me, I nod. "He knows I got on the other train, and this man died because of it. He's taunting me. But it's not just this train. The note says I'm responsible for the train you're on, too. He knows you're on it."

"Show me the note," he says.

I direct the camera at the paper, my eyes sweeping across the words as he reads them.

"'Find one before I hide another,'" I read out loud. "There's another body already, and he's going to kill more."

"Emma, it's more than that—" he starts, but the sound of the sliding door opening pulls my attention away.

I turn toward the door, and my stomach lurches up into my throat. My hand drops, so my phone is no longer pointed at my face. All Sam will be able to see is the carpet and the body a few feet away.

"Emma? Emma, what's going on?" he calls. I slide my thumb across the screen to mute him.

CHAPTER TWENTY-TWO

Positioning myself in the middle of the aisle doesn't do much. There's not enough of me to completely conceal the space behind me, and even if there was, he already saw the body. In those seconds after he opened the door and his eyes locked on me, I was doing nothing to block his view of the end of the aisle. I take a step toward him, holding up a hand to try to calm him.

"Thomas, I need you to listen to me," I start carefully.

The call is muted, but Sam is still on the phone. He can hear everything I'm saying. I want him to know what's happening, so at any second, he can react.

"What the hell is going on here? I told you these cars are empty, blocked off from passengers. What are you doing back here?" he demands.

"Before I explain, I need you to close the door behind you. The fewer people who know what's happened, the better," I tell him.

"Excuse me?" he asks incredulously. "I find you creeping around in a closed car with an obviously injured person, and you're giving me instructions?"

"He's not injured," I say.

It's obvious he hasn't looked closely at the end of the aisle. From his position, the message on the opposite door is concealed, and even the blood is not visible behind me.

"So, he just had a couple too many in the lounge car and is taking a nap?" he scoffs.

"Thomas, he's not injured. This man is dead."

The conductor's face goes pale, and he takes a step back away from me.

"D-dead?" he stammers.

"You can't leave," I say. "Please, you need to stay here with me and let me explain what's going on. You can't let anyone know what's happening right now. It's not safe."

"Are you threatening me?" he asks.

"No. I'm not threatening you, but there's someone else who might. Whoever killed this man could kill someone else. He might already have. And if you go out there and start telling people, then he definitely will. The killer must still be on this train, and we can't tip him off."

"Why should I trust you?" he asks. "Why should I believe anything you say? For all I know, you could have killed him."

"My name is Emma Griffin. I'm with the FBI." I reach into my back pocket for my badge and show him, then I hold up my phone and unmute it. "This is Sam Johnson. He's the sheriff in my town. He's on the other train following this route."

"You're both law enforcement?" Thomas asks, still not sure whether to be suspicious or relieved.

"Yes," Sam tells him. I glance at the screen and see him reach into his pocket to pull out his badge. "Sherwood County Sheriff Sam Johnson. Here. Look."

The conductor looks at the star and gives a tense nod.

"I'm going to step aside and let you look at the body, is that alright?" I ask.

The surprise of the body tumbling out of the vestibule has passed, and I'm no longer uncomfortable with the corpse. My years in the Bureau have made me so familiar with death that I'm just as comfortable with corpses as I am living people. Sometimes more comfortable.

But I'm well aware not everyone has the same level of ease as I do. For many facing a body, especially the victim of a murder, the shock and disgust can be overwhelming. It's not just the body itself, the bluntness of a human devoid of life, or even the injuries. It's the reality of what one person can do to another that's sickening.

I need to be careful with Thomas. His presence in this space is like static electricity. Unstable, sparking. At any second, he could bolt. The train car would swarm with others, and the dangling threat of the sick game, whatever it is, would burst around us. My caution keeps him steady. Holds him in place for another second, another heartbeat. And that means control and safety exist for a heartbeat longer.

He's completely still for a second. I'm not even sure he heard me. I'm about to repeat myself when he finally nods. It's barely perceptible, and his widened eyes don't change, but it's enough for me to take a step back and move to the side. Thomas walks forward to get a better view of the body. The sharp breath pulled into his lungs almost knocks him backwards, and I reach up as if to steady him.

"Do you recognize him?" I ask.

He nods. "He was on the train when I first started my shift. He was supposed to get off at Castleville."

"Do you see how the blood is drying? That takes time. You saw me less than an hour ago. I couldn't have killed him," I explain. "I didn't even get on until Castleville anyway."

He nods again.

My brain completes the thought working in my mind. "And that means we don't necessarily know that the killer is still here. He could have gotten off."

"Show him the note, Emma," Sam says.

I gesture to the note pinned to the body with the knife, then the message on the door, and the one on the tablet.

Thomas listens silently as I explain everything. I leave out some exact details, like the whole history of being undercover in Feathered Nest, but I lead him to believe it's part of a case I'm working. I explain that I switched trains from the ticket sent to me out of caution and tell him that's why I've been keeping an eye on other passengers. When

I'm done, I stare into his face, searching his expression, trying to determine if he's followed anything I said.

"Right now, I don't know what happened or exactly how much danger there actually is. What I can tell you is, this is not something to mess around with. Do you follow me?"

He nods again as if his ability to respond to the situation has devolved down to that one gesture. It's enough. As long as he's interacting, I know he's hearing me and understands what I'm saying.

"At this point, we have to act as responding law enforcement," Sam tells Thomas. "I'll take this train; Emma is in charge there. This situation needs to be kept under close control. The circumstances are very unusual, and in a lot of ways, we're at this guy's mercy. Since we don't know who or even where he is, we can't predict what he's going to do next or prepare for it. There's no way to bring in a team or have backup. We have to do this one step at a time."

Thomas takes a breath. It shudders in his lungs and seems to struggle to come back out. He can't seem to take his eyes away from the body, but the longer he looks at it, the more his expression contorts and his color drains. I step into his line of vision again, giving him the relief of my face blocking his way.

"You can't say anything to anyone," I repeat to him. "As of this moment, you are a part of this investigation. You need to do exactly what we ask of you for the safety of the passengers. If you don't, there could be dire consequences for everyone on this train, and Sam's train. Do you understand?"

"Yes," the conductor finally answers.

"Good. I need you to keep everyone out of this car. No one can come in here. Keep working like you are supposed to, so you don't call attention to yourself, but make sure no one comes into this car."

"Yes," he repeats.

"Good. There's just one more thing I need you to do for me." He nods. "Get me into the baggage car."

"What?" he asks, obviously thrown off by the request.

"I need to get my suitcase, so I can get my gun," I tell him.

"You can't have a gun on board," he says, shaking his head slightly. "It's against regulations for you to carry a firearm on board."

I reach out for his shoulders, gripping them. Sam will now see nothing on his phone but the light blue of Thomas's shirt, but he's slipping. I have to keep control of the situation. I need him to focus on me and make every word get through the storm rolling across his thoughts. Soon the initial shock will wear off, and there will be a crossroads. Either he will be able to handle the pressure of what we're asking of him, or he will crumble. I need him to be present in this moment, to understand the critical importance of shielding the rest of the train from what's happening, so I have a chance.

"Thomas. Thomas, listen to me. I have to have my gun. We don't know what this guy has planned or if he is still on board. If I'm going to be able to do my job and protect everyone on this train, I need my weapon. I packed it in my suitcase. So, I need you to get me into the baggage car to get it. Can you do that?" I ask.

He stares at me, and I keep my eyes trained on him, applying pressure with my hands. I exaggerate my breathing by drawing in long, deep breaths and letting them out slowly. In and out. I guide him into the rhythm. In and out. I force him to focus on nothing but the pressure of my hands and the sound of my breaths. Gradually, his breath matches mine. It slows, calming down, and his shoulders relax. Brought back from the edge, he finally nods.

"It's at the very back of the train, past the sleeper cars. It's locked. You won't make it in. There are too many people in between," he tells me.

"Then you have to do it. I'll stay here." I pull my bag around in front of me and dig through it until I find my bag claim ticket. "Here. It's a black suitcase with a purple luggage tag with my name on it. Emma Griffin. Just bring me the entire thing. Everything is inside."

He looks hesitant, his eyes sliding across the carpet to the pale hand turned palm-up toward the ceiling and a peek of soft belly from where the man's fall pulled his shirt out of place. They move past him, to where the bloodied sliding door offers a movie. He can't see it, but he knows it's there.

"Close your eyes. I'll help you past him," I offer.

"He drank three sodas this morning," Thomas mutters, his voice distant. "One right after the other. Said he didn't like coffee."

I take his wrist and take a step down the aisle in front of him.

"Just close your eyes."

He lets me lead him down the aisle and over the body. I press my back against the edge of the door to force it the rest of the way open, then stand him in the vestibule. The smell of dry blood isn't as strong or fresh, but it's still enough to sting my nose and slide down the back of my throat as I pry open the door. I'm careful not to touch the message and only open it as far as necessary to let him through.

"Is he gone?" Sam asks a few seconds later.

"Yes," I whisper, stepping back into the car.

"Listen to me. It isn't just another body."

"What do you mean?" I ask.

"Emma, there's a bomb."

CHAPTER TWENTY-THREE

S ometimes someone says something to you, and you don't understand it because it's confusing or strangely worded. Sometimes it's because they mumble, or you're not sure you heard exactly what you thought. And sometimes it's because the words are so clear, so unquestionable, they can't possibly be real.

This is one of those moments.

"What the hell do you mean there's a bomb?" I ask. "How do you know that?"

"It's in the note, Emma. Think about the words. It tells you there's another body, but it's not just saying you need to find that one before another dies. Time is ticking. That's what the note says. Time is ticking," Sam points out.

"If the train stops or police show up, you blow it," I mutter. "Christ."

"He's going to blow up the train," Sam says.

"But which one?" I ask. "It says 'your train, your responsibility'."

"Right. So, the train you're on."

"No. The first note says I should have gotten on my train, meaning the one you are on," I point out.

"So, it could be either. Or both."

"How are we supposed to find it? This guy wants to play games, but he's not telling us how."

I let out an exasperated growl.

"Emma, calm down," Sam says.

"Don't tell me to calm down, Sam! A man is dead three feet from me because of a choice I made!"

"It's not your fault."

"Of course it's my fault. I knew there was something going on, that this was dangerous. Not only did I do it anyway, but I changed it. Rather than just following through, I tried to be smart, and a man lost his life," I say.

"And if you hadn't?" Sam asks. "Yes, you knew this was dangerous, but that has never scared you away before. Why should it now? You walk into battle because it's what you were born to do. You know as well as I do if you had gotten on this train, something else would have happened. And if you hadn't gotten on the train at all, he probably had a plan for that too. He could have hurt a lot of other people getting to you."

The words settle in, but they don't sit right with me. I shake my head.

"No." I glance back at the body, then at the screen. "No. That's not what's happening. He could have gotten to me. He obviously knew I was on this train. He knew when I first got on. This man was supposed to get off the train before I got on, so whoever's doing this realized I changed my plans in advance. He killed this man and hid him. Wrote the notes. Everything. When he could have far more easily just come and found me. It's just like he said. He's playing games. He wants to see if I can figure it out."

"Where do we start?"

"The note says we're playing hide and seek. That I have to find one before there's another. Obviously, he's not talking about this man. In order to get the note, I would have already had to find him. So, there's another body. We have to find that in order to stop him from killing somebody else. And maybe it'll lead us to the bomb," I say.

"How are we supposed to know when the bomb is going to go off?

He says time's ticking. Obviously, that means there's a planned deto-nation," Sam points out.

I think about it for a second, shifting my weight back and forth on my feet as I pick through each piece of the note.

"Maybe he already told us. Right there in his warnings. 'If you let the train stop'. We are assuming that means not to call the police and not to call security because they would stop at the next station. But what if it's more than that? What if he means if the train stops for any reason, it'll trigger the explosion?" I suggest.

"Meaning, we can't let the train get to its stop without figuring this out?" Sam completes my thought.

"Exactly. That gives us less than two hours."

"Then we need to get started. Where do we search first?" he asks.

"We need to be careful. We can't alert anyone to something unusual going on. It's enough that Thomas knows about it. If other people find out, somebody is going to contact train security, and they're going to divert the train to the next station. One of the trains will end up getting stopped, and that will put a pretty quick end to us trying to figure out where the bomb is. So, we need to be careful in how we approach this. I don't think he just wants us to search. That's not interesting enough for him. He left me the message on the door that led me to the tablet. He's going to want us to follow his bread-crumbs," I say. "And I don't think it's going to be here."

"What do you mean?"

"The note specifically asks if I can keep a secret, then mentions you. Both trains are involved in this. We already know the bomb could be on either one. The notes could be, too. Are there any empty passenger cars on your train?"

"I doubt it," Sam tells me. "It's pretty full. Most of the seats in my car and all of them between me and the snack car are taken. I don't think they'd have things this packed and leave other cars empty. That's another thing. He has to be on my train."

"Why?" I ask.

"How could he have planted things on both and then be on yours? Your train left the station before mine even got there."

"Do we know he planted things on both cars, though? Have you found anything?"

"Not yet, but I'll start a sweep as soon as we hang up."

I whip around toward the sound of the door opening and see Thomas climbing gingerly over the body. He has my suitcase gripped to his stomach, pressed against him as if to protect it. When he's inside, he carries it over to me and sets it at my feet.

"Did anyone see you?" I ask.

The conductor shakes his head. "No. There weren't any attendants in the sleeper cars, and the baggage car was empty when I got to it."

"Perfect," I say, kneeling down and flipping the suitcase over so I can open it.

The tiny metal discs on the padlock click into place as I align my code.

7 - 22 - 91.

The top flips over onto the floor, and I move the layer of clothes I put on top of my gun case. Thomas's breath catches in his throat as he watches me put my gun back together and load it. My harness on my hip and my gun tucked securely into it; I pull my sweatshirt down over it.

"Thomas, you told me these cars are empty because they were where the people who got off in Castleville were sitting, right?" I ask.

"Yes. The leg of the journey from Castleville through to the last stop in Virginia wasn't going to have many passengers, so we closed off these cars. It doesn't make much sense to have several cars with just one or two people, especially when we're expecting a large influx of passengers carrying on to the Carolinas, Georgia, and Florida."

"So, everyone who is in the cars up toward the front of the train got on in Castleville?" I ask.

"No," he shakes his head. "There are a few passengers who have been with us since New York. They were sent into those passenger cars in preparation for emptying these. It just makes it easier to have empty cars when there's going to be a large number of passengers boarding so that they can be arranged."

"Arranged?" I raise an eyebrow, remembering my conversation

with Eric. "So, at the next stop, the passengers who get on there will have assigned seats?"

"Yes," Thomas says. "It can get extremely complicated when there are several groups as well as individuals. People very rarely position themselves in the most logical ways, and it can create complications and wasted space."

"They like the control," I say. "They want to be able to choose something for themselves."

"Yes. One of the things we see most frequently is actually what you did when you boarded. You sat down in the window seat and put your bag in the seat beside you. You moved it under your seat, but the first thing you did was put it beside you. That took up that whole aisle. That's fine in situations like the car you're in because there aren't so many passengers that taking up that extra seat creates a problem. But when the cars will be mostly full, and there are groups to accommodate, that creates a hassle."

"It's like a game of Tetris," Sam adds.

"In a way," the conductor agrees, seemingly thankful to focus on the minutia of his job rather than the dead body behind him. "We have to look at the different groups and families, and ensure they are able to sit together first. We arrange them in the most effective ways to spread them out, so we don't end up with several large groups right on top of each other, but also so the seats can be used effectively. Once we have that arranged, we put couples in, then fill in with singles."

"And people aren't allowed to move seats?" I ask.

"They're discouraged from it. Moving their seat can throw off the entire seating arrangement. Sometimes we have plans for a group coming on at the next stop, and if someone moves seats, it can disrupt that. When that's a potential issue, we do additional sweeps to check and make sure everyone is still seated where they are supposed to be."

My eyes widen.

"My seat," I say.

"What?" both men ask.

"My seat. My original seat on the other train. I didn't switch my ticket. I bought a new one for this train. That means my old seat should have been assigned. Would the conductor fill in my seat with someone else once they went through and noticed I wasn't there?"

"Unlikely. It would probably just remain open just in case you missed the train but boarded at another stop. Or were somewhere else in the train and had to be moved back to where you were supposed to be sitting," he tells me.

"Sam, you need to try to find my seat. The one that was assigned to me," I tell him.

"Alright. I'll call you back."

I hang up and look at Thomas.

"You need to tell me about Mr. Jones."

CHAPTER TWENTY-FOUR

"M r. Jones?" Thomas asks, confused. "Why would you want to know about him?"

"He hasn't been seen since before the train started," I say. "And he looked nervous as hell when he was getting on."

"He always looks like that," the conductor explains. "That's just how he is."

"So, he does ride frequently?"

"Frequently enough. Every couple of weeks."

"And he goes all the way to Georgia? Isn't that kind of a far way to go that often?" I ask. "What's he going there for?"

"I've never gotten that in-depth in my conversations with him. I know his name because I look at his ticket. He sits in the same seat every time," he offers.

"And he sits there and reads? Like he was doing while we were waiting for the train to start?" I ask.

"He always has a book. I've never seen him on a tablet or even his phone. He comes in and sits, takes out his book. He always looks just slightly uncomfortable. I don't know if it's because he doesn't like to travel or because he doesn't like whatever's waiting for him in Georgia," Thomas says.

"Don't you find it odd that he's missing?"

"I told you before; he's not missing."

"Do you want me to believe he's been doing laps of the train for more than two hours, and I just happened to not have noticed him? He wasn't in the snack car, or in any of the cars leading to it. He wasn't in any of the other cars. There's a body here, Thomas."

"And he doesn't have anything to do with it," the conductor says quickly.

"You know that? Somehow you are absolutely positive about it?" I ask.

"Yes."

"How? First, you barely even know the man, but now you're so fast to defend him?"

"You can't possibly think he murdered this man," Thomas says, his voice lower and more controlled now. "He rides this train all the time. I have seen him over and over. There was nothing different about him today than there has been any other time he's boarded."

"Except that he disappeared."

My phone rings for a video chat, and I swipe my finger across it to open it.

"Sam?"

"I found it," he whispers.

He's moving down the aisle with the phone held close to his face.

"The seat I was supposed to be sitting in?" I ask.

"Yes. Give me just a second," he says. I wait while he continues through the car, then see him pass through the sliding door into the snack car. "I wanted to get somewhere without so many people to hear what I'm saying," he explains.

"The snack car? Really?"

"It's just the guy behind the counter, and he is far more invested in his phone right now than he is in anything around him. I don't even know if he realizes I came in here," Sam whispers.

"Good. Keep it that way. What did you find?"

"The conductors wouldn't tell me where you were assigned to sit. They said it was a privacy and security issue. So, I remembered what you said about finding the green note inside your computer, and I started looking at the tags above people's seats."

"Green note?" Thomas asks.

I fish the paper out of my pocket and show it to him.

"When I went to the snack car, I put my computer in my bag, under the seat. Just like you saw. But when I came back, my bag was still under the seat, but my computer was sitting on the tray table. I opened it and found this stuck to the screen."

"It must have been his," he surmises.

"Exactly," Sam nods. "So, I looked at the tags for the different destinations. I figured with the train as busy as it is, it's unlikely there are going to be a lot of people going to the same place scattered across all the cars. You said, for the most part, you like to keep people fairly well contained. So, I started in my car, but there weren't any empty seats. I went to the next one and saw an empty seat, but the person sitting beside it told me there was someone there, just in the bathroom. It took a little while of wandering up and down the train, but I realized someone moved. Her tag didn't fit in with the ones around her. When I asked her about it, she thought it was my seat and admitted moving. She was willing to go back to her original seat if I wanted to sit there; she just wanted to be somewhere quieter."

"Did you make her move?" I ask.

"Of course I did. There was no one in the seat beside her, which is precisely why she moved into that spot."

"There was going to be an empty seat beside me?" I frown. "That's odd."

"See, that's the thing. I noticed the conductor coming by right as she was leaving, so I sat down. He made a comment about telling that girl she needed to move, and that I was going to have to, too. He needed me in my correct seat. I asked if the seat next to your assigned one was available, and he said no. That both seats were assigned," Sam says.

"Both of them were assigned, and both of them were empty?" Thomas asks. "That is odd."

"Not if they were bought together," I point out. "You said yourself groups are seated together as much as possible when there's assigned seating. If the tickets were purchased together, the conductor would assign them seats together. The ticket I got in the mail was a hard ticket, like one bought directly from the train station rather than online. If you buy them online, you get the confirmation email, and it says how many passengers are traveling together. But not if you get the hard ticket. Just looking at my ticket wouldn't show that another ticket was purchased at the same time."

"So, whoever sent you the ticket bought themselves one, too. Either they just wanted to make sure you would be on the same train so they could find you. Or they knew enough about the routes to know the later train is the busier one and more likely to have assigned seats," Sam points out.

"That doesn't explain how he knew I wasn't on that train. If he waited until he got on the train and saw I wasn't there, it would be long after this train left. He murdered a man well before that train even got to the station. There was some other way he knew I wasn't getting on that train."

I let out a breath, then remember why Sam went looking for my seat. "Did you find anything at the seat?"

"Yes. After the conductor left, I went back to the seat and looked around. I sat down to try to be at your perspective. It took me a minute, but then I saw them."

"Them?" I ask.

Sam nods and sets his hand palm-down on the table in front of him, turning the camera so I can see. He moves his hand away, and I see two tiny sparkling silver balls on posts.

"They were embedded in the back of the seat in front of you," Sam explains, "right at your eye level. You couldn't have missed them."

"Earrings?" I ask.

"That's what they look like."

"Why would there be earrings in the back of the seat?" Thomas asks. "How did no one notice someone putting them there?"

"They blended in with the seat really well. And since no one was sitting there, they must not have stood out. Whoever put them there must have gotten into the car before the other passengers, or when there were only a few. They put them in and then left without calling attention to themselves," Sam explains.

"Was there anything else?" I ask.

"I didn't see anything."

"Did you check the pocket on the back of the seat? Or the overhead compartment?"

"Not the overhead compartment."

His hand swipes the earrings from the surface of the table as he stands and heads out of the snack car back toward the passenger car. The angle he carries the phone lets me see the faces of the passengers as he passes their seats. Several glance up, registering him, then go back to what they are doing. A few pay closer attention, watching him until he's several rows away. I watch each carefully, seeing if any seem to have a particular interest in him. One woman tilts her head to watch him for longer, but I don't notice anyone who immediately strikes me as suspicious.

When he gets back to the row of seats, Sam turns the camera around so I can see what he sees. Bags press in on either side of the overhead compartment from the space on either side, but the center portion seems empty. He holds up the phone a little higher, and I catch a glimpse of something bright pink.

"What is that?" I ask. "In the back?"

Sam reaches inside and pulls the object forward. He brings it down and holds it in front of the camera. The bright pink envelope has my name written across it in the same handwriting dripping blood on the door behind me. Turning the camera around again, he heads back to the snack car.

"People are starting to pay more attention to what I'm doing," he mutters as he sits back down. "I have to be careful."

"What's in the envelope?"

His fingers dip into the envelope and pulls out a card. He turns it around to face the camera.

"Happy Sweet Sixteen," I whisper.

CHAPTER TWENTY-FIVE

ANSON

FIVE MONTHS EARLIER...

He had no idea how long it would be before his name was really his again. That was one of the things he thought about as the months crept on, and his plans took form in his mind. There was more, of course, but some days, when the details weren't falling into place when he was waiting for something to happen, he thought about his name. Sometimes he said it to himself, feeling it fill his mouth and fall through his teeth like hot tea. Sometimes he pretended to hear someone else calling him by it. It had been a long time since he heard it and he didn't know how he would feel to hear it again.

When he first crossed the path of Lotan, Anson was the only name he'd ever known. He didn't grow up with a nickname, something shortened or made more approachable with a 'y'. His father didn't even call him Sonny. The name he was born into was the name he was called. But Lotan changed that. He welcomed him. He seemed to appreciate him. He showed him a world Anson never knew. Taught him things he could never have imagined. Lotan helped him shed the image of the world he had been holding onto throughout his life, so he could step into a greater, more powerful, more impactful existence. And he gave him a new name.

Anson cherished that name. It meant everything to him to be seen as worthy. As valuable enough to earn the name he was given. He saw it as so much more than a name. It was a title. An acknowledgement of who he was among the ranks.

At first, he felt like part of a wave, flowing together, strong and mighty. There was the crest, peaking at the top and turning to virulent foam before the crash; and there was the trough, the unseen and sometimes overlooked power. But it was all one. Over time, that changed. He went from part of the wave to dissolved salt and now realized he was nothing but a grain of sand on the beach.

The wave was still there, of course. Leviathan dwelled in the brutal force of the waves. There could be no Leviathan without that force. But Anson was no longer a part of it. Most of them weren't. They were sand scattered on the beach, waiting for the touch of water. That's when he first started to think of his name again. It didn't feel as much like he was given something, but rather that something was taken away.

Maybe that's when he started thinking more about Emma. She gave people back their names. That stood out to him. He watched her face on the news, read about her in every way he could. Any time she was mentioned, he absorbed it because he needed to understand. He needed some insight into who she was and why she mattered so much.

She didn't like the flash of the journalists' cameras. She didn't want the microphones in her face. Not on the news and not in court. Even when she was standing there, stoic and in control, it was obvious. She didn't want them looking at her, attempting to dismantle her so they could lay out what she did in neat little pieces, consumable bites easy for the public. In that way, she was so much like Lotan.

There are things that shouldn't be easy. Life shouldn't always come in the simplest form. That's what leads to complacency and mediocrity. It's what leads to being trampled.

Anson believed in those things. He felt them within him like they were stitched into the fibers that crafted him. He had never put voice to them until he met Lotan. Never knew the words. But he gave himself completely once he understood.

Until he realized that would never be enough. He would try. He would push. He would do everything he thought he could, and it would still never be enough. Because she's the only one who ever mattered. The only one Lotan never renamed.

Emma gave people their names back. Even when it was only to etch them into their gravestones, she made sure their names were known. She spoke them and wrote them. She kept them a part of the universe so they couldn't be forgotten again. Hearing that is what truly made Anson understand. It's what changed everything for him.

He didn't want Emma to give him his name back. He didn't need her to. He would have it for himself. But she was the reason he didn't know if he would ever be able to feel fully comfortable with just one name again. There wasn't a single part of him, a single thought that strayed away from what he believed. He wasn't drawn into Leviathan because of anything less than true and unwavering belief in the mission. But that wasn't the way it was anymore. The mission fell out of favor, and she took its place as his treasured focus. Anson could never feel like he did before Lotan came along. He was changed, fully, and irreparably. He also wasn't a grain of sand.

Soon he would rise. Thoughts that had existed only in the back of his mind for so long washed up to the surface. He couldn't ignore them anymore. His quiet work had built what would become the opening salvo of his legacy. It was nearly complete. Just a few more pieces, a few more adjustments, and he would restore the mission. Disrupt the god of chaos.

The sound of his computer brought him away from the pieces of metal that pressed into his fingers, drawing drops of blood from his skin like they were getting their first tastes. That metal would soon have so much more. He looked at the screen, and a smile twitched at his lips. The message was just what he hoped it would be. She thought she was brilliant, and he would tell her she was. She thought the ideas were hers, and he would praise her for them.

Anything to get her there.

Lotan had plans. Anson had better ones. Lotan was sending a wave. Anson would create a tsunami.

He was tired of toiling away in the background, having no say. No glory. Bowing down to a man who chased shadows and corpses for nearly twenty years.

Now it was his turn.

CHAPTER TWENTY-SIX

NOW

"Happy Sweet Sixteen," I say again. "I don't understand. What the hell is that supposed to mean?"

Sam looks at the camera and shakes his head.

"I don't know."

"What's inside? Does it say anything?" I ask.

"Emma," Thomas starts from beside me. "I can't stay here for much longer. The rest of the staff is going to notice."

I look at him, feeling almost like I'd forgotten he was even there.

"You're right. You don't want anything to seem strange or call any attention to what's going on. We need to keep things as normal as possible. Go back and do whatever it is you need to be doing. But make sure no one is suspicious of you and no one tries to come back here. You understand?"

"I understand," he nods. "Are you going to stay here?"

The breath slides out of my lungs, and I realize I don't really have an answer for that.

"I can't stay here for the entire time," I tell him. "I have to try to figure out what these clues mean. That means looking around the train. But we can't risk anyone coming in here and finding the body. No security. No police. It's far too dangerous to call his bluff. This guy keeps his promises, and the last thing we want to know is just how fast he can do it."

"Until we are almost at the station, there's no reason for anybody to come into these cars. They have already been cleaned and are just waiting for the next passengers."

"Then why did you come back here?" I ask. "If nobody's supposed to be in these cars, why did you end up back here to find me?"

"Exactly what you just said. To find you. You were roaming up and down the cars asking about Mr. Jones, and I had the feeling something was going on."

"Well, we have to make sure no one else has that feeling. I will check back in here as often as I can, but my top priority is figuring out where he's leading me next, so I can try to stop whatever he has planned. If I need your help, I'll come find you."

Thomas nods and leaves the car. I watch him, shaking my head as he goes.

"What is it?" Sam asks.

"There's something about him," I mutter, making sure to not be overheard. "I don't know what it is, but there's something he isn't being upfront about."

"You don't think he's the one who did this, do you?" he asks.

"No," I say. "But there's something about the way he was talking about that other passenger that's bothering me."

"He just said that he doesn't know him very well, but sees him on the train pretty often," Sam tells me.

"Right, but he was very quick to defend him. Not just to say he didn't think he would have anything to do with it, but to intensely deny it. There's no reason to think Mr. Jones killed this man or could be responsible for the clues. I don't know him, and I have no reason to believe he knows me. He sat there beside me and didn't acknowledge me. Whoever wrote these notes knows me."

"Then why are you concerned about Thomas telling you he has nothing to do with it?" Sam asks.

"Because I never mentioned thinking he could have murdered this man. All I did was point out he stood up and walked away from his seat while we were still delayed and didn't come back."

"Like he could be the next one," Sam says, realizing what I'm trying to get across.

"Exactly. But Thomas jumped right into insisting he couldn't have anything to do with this. Like it wasn't a surprise to him that he wasn't in his seat, kind of like he would have no reason to be worried about him," I say. "And for him to chase me down just because of that man in the first place? Very odd."

"What do you think that means?" he asks.

"I don't know. But it's something to keep in mind. Right now, I need to concentrate on that card and what it means. Is there anything written inside?"

Sam opens the card and shows it to me.

"'Check your list,'" he reads. "'Can you catch me?'"

"Check my list. What list? What could that be talking about?" I ask.

"It's a birthday card, so maybe it has something to do with that. A guest list, like for a party?"

"The passenger list? I'll see if Thomas has access to it and could give it to me. But it can't be that simple. What do we think is going to happen? We'll look at the list, and one of the names will be high-lighted, and it'll say caught me? I want to look up with the names, but there are plenty of other ways he could have led us to a passenger list. And it's not *my* list. It says to check my list. Why would he choose a birthday card?" I ask.

"You said somebody was at your seat. They took your computer out of its bag and put it on the table," Sam says.

"Yes. That's how I found the sticky note for the seat where this man was sitting," I tell him.

"Did you look anywhere else?" he asks. "Could whoever it was who took the computer out have left something else at your seat?"

"It was a woman," I say. "I haven't thought about that until you just said that. The guy sitting a couple of rows behind me said he saw a woman at my seat. Don't you remember me telling you that? Blonde hair and a blue sweater. Apparently similar enough to me that he didn't think anything of seeing her there."

"So, it's possible we are not looking for a man. We're looking for a woman," Sam notes.

"Or two people," I say. "This whole time we've been wondering how this person could have gone back and forth between the trains, but what if they didn't? One on your train, one on mine."

"Can you think of anyone you know who fits that description? Someone who might want to do something like this?"

"No. But I'm going to see if I can find out more about her. I'll check around my seat and talk to that man again. I need you to do something for me," I say.

"What is it?"

"Go on the Feathered Nest website and look up the handyman named Clancy. He's probably the only one listed. He works for the town managing their buildings and properties," I say.

"Alright. Why am I calling him?" Sam asks.

"Tell him you are calling for me, and that I want him to go check in on Marren for me."

"Okay."

"I just want to make sure she's alright. She obviously didn't send me that letter, and I want to make sure she's safe," I explain. "I can't call LaRoche again. No police, remember? Just ask him to check on her, and I'll go check my seat. I'll talk to you soon."

The call ends, and the time glows on my screen. My chest burns with the urgency creeping up. We're getting closer and closer to the station, and I have no clue what else I'll have to unravel. I glance down at myself to make sure my gun is concealed, and I haven't picked up any traces of blood. Satisfied, I leave my suitcase where it is, sling my backpack on my back again, and walk out into the first empty car.

I know it's just my imagination, but this car feels brighter, and there seems to be more air in it than the last car. I've gotten so used to the smell of blood that the full breaths of cold, filtered air seem cleansing as they draw through my lungs and take away the heaviness. My expression changes with each step. I force my shoulders down. I release the tension in my muscles. My eyes open slightly to stop my eyebrows from furrowing. It's a systematic change, my concentration fully on making each feature look relaxed and at ease so that when I step out in front of people again, they won't notice me moving among them.

Act like you belong. No one will question you. It's the simplest tip of being undercover, but sometimes the most difficult. When you already feel like you don't belong or are standing out in a situation, it's easy to slip. You start to exaggerate behaviors meant to help you blend in or look anxious and give yourself away. That's one of the first ways I can always tell an agent who has never gone undercover.

But I'm used to it. I've lent my existence to many different personas over the years and, with few exceptions, managed to sink into those lives. Even more importantly, I've found my way back to myself after each and every one of them.

CHAPTER TWENTY-SEVEN

The cars seem largely unchanged as I walk back through them toward my seat. I notice Thomas ahead of me, leaned over as a passenger talks to him. His eyes slide over to me, but his expression doesn't change, and he turns his attention back to the woman. She has a map in her hand and seems extremely concerned. I glance down at the blue-eyed man as I walk past his seat toward mine. He's still hunched over his sketch pad, this time smudging the lines of a drawing with his thumb. The position of his arm and the angle of his head blocks most of the drawing, so I can't see what it is.

The seat where I was sitting and the one next to it are still empty. A quick glance across the aisle proves that seat is as well. Trying not to call any attention to myself, I quickly scan the area. I take my time pulling my backpack off my back and setting it on the seat, so I have a few extra seconds to look at the surrounding rows and the floor beneath the seats in front of me. I don't notice anything tucked there, and I reach up to open the overhead compartment.

Just like the one I saw over the video call with Sam, the overhead compartment is empty. Grateful for my height, I rise up on the balls of my feet to get a better look inside. Glancing both ways, I don't see anything until several rows ahead. I sit down and scan the backs of the seats, paying close attention to every inch of the blue and gray fabric.

"Check your list," I whisper to myself.

Several pieces of paper stick out of the mesh pouch on the seat in front of me, and I pull them out. I sift through each of them, looking for anything written on them or stuck to them. It's nothing but the usual advertisements and magazines stuffed there to give passengers hungry to fill the long hours of a train trip with any type of distraction.

I glance up in time to see Thomas step away from the woman and start his slow stroll down the aisle. Pulling open my bag, I take out a small notepad and pen I always bring with me. I scribble a note asking Thomas for the passenger list and fold it up, setting it on the arm of the seat where I hope he'll see it. My phone rings as I toss the pen and pad away. I'm expecting to see Sam's name on the screen, but it's Bellamy.

"Hey, B," I say.

"Hey, you alright?" she asks.

I briefly consider telling her what's happening, but I stop myself. As unorthodox as this situation is, I have to consider it an investigation. Sam is involved by default, but the fewer people who know what's happening, the less the chance of it being compromised. And for all I know, our suspect could be listening in very intently. If I let anyone know, I'd, well, blow it.

"I'm fine. Just on the train."

"Eric said you wanted me to look into that guy's profile for you," she says, and the conversation rushes back.

"Right," I say, keeping my voice low. I still don't want to draw too much attention to myself. "I thought you might be able to look over it and point out anything that strikes you as odd or unusual. I know you're not going to be able to go as in-depth as usual, but just a glance would help. I mean, for all I know, it's a completely legit profile, and I'm just missing the deeper meaning of it."

"No," she says. "I looked at it, and I think it's strange, too. Obviously, I've seen plenty of people who think they're really smart or creative and want to share that with all of humanity. But that's not the vibe I'm getting from this. It's too... manufactured. I'm not sure if that's exactly the right word, but it's the best way I can describe it. There's weird artsy bohemian stuff, and then there's someone being too strategic. That's what this profile feels like to me. It's trying too hard. But still, that might just be the person. They've seen a lot of profiles they think are artsy or impressive and are trying to emulate them. They want to create a particular feel but don't quite have the nuance down. Or it could be intentional."

This is far from the first time Bellamy has delved into social media as part of an investigation. Part of her consultancy work for the Bureau includes social media forensics, using technology, and a person's use of platforms to better understand them as individuals. This is often an extremely effective way to bring context to crimes or find missing pieces that bring together a far larger picture of a person and their involvement in people and events around them. I'm always amazed by how much she's able to draw out of seemingly tiny details.

"What do you think about the name?" I ask.

"It's odd," she says. "Not that it immediately tells me anything. What people choose as their names on social media is pretty often an adventure into the absurd. For every person who uses their real government name, there are twenty others who try to be clever or mysterious. This one follows a pattern. Each of the main words rhymes. That could be the intention of using 'he' rather than 'him', though it is an odd choice if it's supposed to reference boyfriend or husband. But, again, it fits with the rhyming scheme. It's strange though. The name says 'at sea'. See at sea. That sounds like boating. And there are a few pictures that could be taken from a boat, but the vast majority of them were taken from shore. The person isn't at sea. They're at *the sea*. There's a difference. So, why would the user take some serious liberties with grammar to fit in with a pattern they like, but then leave out a word that actually does fit?"

"Can you put together a sketch of a person based on that name?" I ask.

She makes a sound that tells me she's not completely convinced.

"That's kind of touchy territory. Just because usernames are so easily changed, and they can mean different things depending on the platform and why it's used. I mean, for all we know, it could just be someone coming up with a silly rhyme. But if I was just handed this name and had to come up with the first stock image person that came to mind, it would probably be a woman in her late teens or early twenties who was really into sailing or, more likely, yachting. That is what I like to affectionately refer to as a basic bitch bullshit username. It makes very little sense but sounds impressive if you just say it and move on. But here's the thing... that's not what I get from the profile. They don't match."

"They don't?"

"The profile feels like a man made it. Again, not an exact science. But there are a few things I pick up online when I look at profiles, and this one has more of a masculine perspective to it. It feels older than the name implies as well. This isn't the perspective of a young woman who loves the ocean. There's no joy in these pictures. She isn't trying to capture the light of a romantic sunset or even a really magnificent wave. If we're going with my original perspective of the type of person who would have a name like that, there are no images of boats, none of the usual things you would expect. No ubiquitous painted toenail picture or even a book and a bottle of wine in the sand. No pictures of herself, either. Now, that could mean she's just a private person, but on top of everything else, it sticks out. There are these patterns and trends that show up across profiles from certain demographics that fit in with interests and hobbies. This one doesn't really make sense with any of them. Yes, there is that shadow of a man, but it... it doesn't tell a story. Does that make sense?"

"It actually does," I say. "How about the captions or the comments?"

"There aren't a lot, actually. Not much interaction at all. A few words here and there, but for the most, comments are turned off. Nobody is able to interact," she says. "It doesn't feel like a personal profile at all—almost more of a random curation of photos, but this is not a photographer's work either. And still, that doesn't explain the interactions with Mary Preston."

"That's interesting." I think about this for a few seconds, but no conclusions immediately gel. "Thank you for doing that for me, B."

"Absolutely. Any time. Have you heard anything else from Christina?" she asks.

"Not yet. I'm hoping she comes back from Florida soon. I want to go talk to her and see if she has anything else for me," I tell her.

"You never heard anything from the funeral home?" she asks.

"Nope," I sigh. "They were as receptive to me asking questions as they were to you. Even when I told them I'm her daughter, they wouldn't talk."

"I'll keep trying. Whatever I can do."

"I know you will. Thank you. When I have ten seconds to breathe, I'm going to come to town, and we're going to spend a weekend in our pajamas, eating pizza, and watching a marathon of all the terrible TV we've been missing," I tell her.

"That sounds amazing," she chuckles.

"Miss you."

"Miss you too. Be safe."

As soon as the call ends, the levity of talking to my best friend drains out of me, and reality sinks in again. I walk out of my row and down the aisle to sit in the seat across from the man drawing. He looks up at me, and I notice the flecks of paler color in his eyes. Like broken glass scattered over water.

He speaks before I'm able to.

"What branch of law enforcement are you?"

CHAPTER TWENTY-EIGHT

"**E**xcuse me?" I ask.

"What branch of law enforcement are you?" he repeats.

"Are you approached by law enforcement so frequently that's become your go-to opener for any conversation?" I raise an eyebrow.

He lets out a short laugh, but there's little humor behind it.

"Not exactly. I'm a private investigator. Watching people and figuring them out is kind of my thing. Everybody has a tell," he explains.

"And I have a law enforcement tell?" I ask.

He nods slowly. I glare at those shards of glass, my mind trying to piece them back together to see if they'll give me a glimpse into him. Being near him is disquieting. He's guarded, and his immediate launch into questioning me is a way to deflect any effort I might put into finding out more about him. He offered the tidbit of being a private investigator as both an explanation of his prying, and a token, to make me feel like he's giving just as much as he's asking. Of course, that's almost never the case.

"You do," he nods. "I just can't pin down what it means."

"Well, whether I'm law enforcement or not doesn't really matter.

I'm not traveling for any official business of any kind. I'm actually on my way to visit a friend. But I did have a question for you," I say.

His eyes flick up and down my face like he's evaluating me. He obviously didn't get out of me what he wanted, and now we're at a stalemate. I don't have any reason not to tell him I'm an agent—but he doesn't have any reason to know. The fact that he asked is what stops me from answering him.

"Go ahead," he finally says.

"The woman you saw at my seat. What can you tell me about her? Other than she had blonde hair and you thought it was me?"

"That's really it. I didn't notice her go to your seat or anything. I wasn't paying that much attention, to be honest. I happened to look up and see her. That's it."

That isn't the answer I was hoping for. I was depending on him being able to give me some other detail to point me in the right direction. I also realize that coming from a supposed private investigator, it's probably a steaming pile of poop. But I keep myself level.

"Alright," I say. "Thanks."

"Don't I get to ask you a question in return?" he asks.

"You already did," I reply.

"Another one. Where have you been?"

I don't like the way he asks it, or the way he's looking at me. It's more than curiosity. There's a note in his voice that sounds oddly like entitlement.

"Nowhere," I tell him.

Thomas crosses in between us at that moment, slicing through the tension I hadn't even realized was there. This isn't sparking tension like between Sam and me when we first saw each other again when I returned to Sherwood. Or heated tension like the lingering undercurrent of battle with LaRoche. This feels more like the two sides of a piece of Velcro being ripped apart. We're each trying to pull something out of the other one and are unwilling to say exactly what.

I glance up at the conductor to see his eyes burning down at me. They swing to face in front of him as he continues on down the aisle, the sway of his body slightly faster than when he was just scanning over tickets and giving his cursory check-ins before. There's some-thing folded in his back pocket. I want to immediately hop up and chase after him, but I force myself to hesitate.

Every set of eyes that would watch me follow after him would be another set of eyes more likely to watch every one of my movements. Building curiosity is what leads to disaster. Panic doesn't always happen instantly. It starts as noticing one small thing and grows with each new detail, whether they mean anything or not. Often more when they don't. I need to keep the rest of the people on this train, not noticing I'm here. It's the only way I'm going to be able to move through and do what needs to be done.

As Thomas continues up the aisle, I walk away from the private investigator and go back to my seat. I spend a few seconds absently digging through my bag, then put it over my shoulder and start up the aisle. He's waiting for me just beyond the next car, in the vestibule between it and the next passenger car. The folded papers from his back pocket slip into my bag, and he leans close.

"I don't think I have to tell you I'm not supposed to give those to you. I'm not even really supposed to have all of them," he whispers.

"And I don't think I have to tell you the possibility of stopping a serial murderer supersedes train passenger confidentiality," I tell him.

He nods solemnly. "Have you figured it out yet?"

"Not unless the answer is spelled out on this," I tell him. "I'll let you know."

He passes back into the passenger car as I move towards the snack car and sit at one of the tables the way Sam did. My position ensures I can look over the entire car and see the door, so no one will be able to surprise me. If anyone else comes into the car, I can quickly conceal the list. I go to work reading over the names, hoping one stands out to me. I see my own, but none of the others sound familiar.

I read it again, looking for patterns. One name swims to the surface. Dean Steele. It makes me pause. I've seen that name before. I'm trying to remember exactly where, when something else on the papers grabs my attention.

The shock shoots through me and makes the tips of my fingers tingle. I'm up and heading back through the train before I can finish dialing Sam. Thomas has stopped patrolling and sits in one of the front seats of the passenger car, a deck of cards forgotten in his hand as he stares out the window beside him at the landscape rushing past.

"Excuse me," I say, keeping my voice steady.

"Emma?" Sam answers, but I keep my focus on Thomas.

He looks up at me, and I slightly widen my eyes.

"There's a problem with my seat. Do you think you could help me?" I ask. The conductor nods and sets his cards down so he can follow me. I purposely walk him directly to my row and gesture toward my seat. "You see, my computer was in my bag, and when I came back, it was on the table. I looked over things and noticed something I was missing."

Thomas and I meet eyes, and he nods.

"I apologize, ma'am. If you'll come with me, I can have you fill out a report, and we'll see what we can do," he says.

We walk in silence through the next two passenger cars and into the silence of the first empty one.

"What did you figure out, Emma?" Sam asks.

"Did you actually mean you missed something or was that just to distract people?" Thomas asks.

"We really did miss something. And thank you for going along with that so smoothly. That guy sitting a few rows behind me is a little squirrely, and I need to throw him off as much as possible," I tell him. "But I had to get to you. Thomas, I need you to get me into the baggage car."

"The baggage car?" he asks, sounding confused. "I already got your suitcase. Did you check something else?"

"Listen to what you just said," I point out. "What do most people do before going on a trip when they want to make sure they don't forget anything?"

"Make a packing list," Sam says as the realization dawns on him.

"And when you get to the train station, you hand your bags over, and they check your list."

Thomas's eyes widen, and we set off through the empty car. I push

154

him ahead of me as we approach the body, keeping my hand pressed to his back. We pass through the third empty car and to the door that leads into the first sleeper car. It's still and quiet. I tense slightly, waiting for someone to walk through one of the doors, or an attendant to appear at the end of the aisle. We keep going, moving faster now, breaking into a run once we reach the second sleeper car. It seems they won't end, that the train keeps multiplying and building on itself. But finally, we get to a solid door.

Thomas unlocks the door, and we step into a final vestibule. A sign across the door marks it as the baggage car, for employees only.

"I'll go in and make sure no one is there," Thomas says.

The unstable metal plates shake and toss beneath my feet as the train rattles on, making my wait feel endless. Finally, he opens the door again and gestures me inside.

CHAPTER TWENTY-NINE

I can't think of a time in my life when I have actively tried to imagine what a baggage car in a train looks like. In fact, if someone had asked me a week ago where luggage was kept during train rides, I probably would have told them a hatch on the side of the train pops up and they toss the bags inside like they do on buses. My experience with checking luggage on trains has always ended with turning in my ticket and claiming my bags inside the station, never with watching them actually remove the bags from the train.

It makes far more sense when I step inside the car and see it lined on either side with metal cages and racks holding various pieces of luggage in place.

"Do you see anything?" Sam asks.

"No," I tell him. "I'm going to switch you to video."

His face appears on the screen, and a hint of emotion hits the back of my throat.

"Look around," he says. "Pay attention to everything."

"Maybe we should start with where your luggage was," Thomas suggests.

He walks over to one of the cages and gestures. I look at the other luggage, examining each of the shelves and every tag, but nothing seems out of the ordinary. It's mostly rolling bags and a few hard-sided cases.

"We can't open them all," I muse. "There has to be some way to figure out what I'm supposed to be looking for."

"Are you positive it's on your train?" Sam offers. "Remember, it could be in either one. That clue showed up in this one, so maybe it's supposed to lead me to the baggage car here."

"It's possible," I say, walking down the row and scouring every bag and every corner. "But I really doubt it. I know the clue was on that train, but the card specifically said check your list. It was addressed to me. Whoever this is might consider that one my original train and my responsibility, but they would know if I was going to check luggage, it would be in this baggage car. Not the one over there. Besides, there's no way you're going to get into that car without drastic measures. We need to exhaust everything we can before bringing anybody else into this."

"You're right," he nods. "So, I guess all we can do is keep looking."

I stand in the middle of the car and look around at everything. Even with as few passengers as I saw on the train, the amount of luggage seems daunting. In addition to the bags and cases organized on the shelves, there are crates tucked in the corners and several metal boxes lined up on one end.

"What's all that?" I ask Thomas.

"There are three passengers who are moving several states away. They have their luggage, but also brought some of their other belongings with them."

"So, we can probably rule out the crates that belong to them. What else? What don't you recognize?" I ask.

He shakes his head. "I'm not the one who checks the baggage. This isn't my car. I have access to it, but I don't have any idea what belongs to who. That's why there are claim tickets."

I look around at the various boxes and containers again and an idea comes to mind. I dig the passenger list out of my pocket and point out where it indicates which passengers checked luggage.

"We can go over the list and compare it to the containers that are here. Maybe one of them isn't accounted for," I suggest.

We start going over the list, passenger by passenger, taking note of which ones checked luggage and which didn't. I quickly realize there isn't an indication of what they checked, but rather how many pieces. We are halfway down the list when I notice something different next to one of the names. I point to it.

"What's this?" I ask.

"That person checked a bike," Thomas explains. "Some trains allow passengers to bring bikes on board and put them up in the area by the disability seating. But this particular train doesn't have that option. People who have bikes with them have to check them just like luggage."

"I don't see any bikes in here," I point out. "Are they kept somewhere else?"

He shakes his head. "No. They're right there."

He points to the metal boxes. The odd shape initially made me think they might contain drums or equipment of some kind.

"Some people don't want to break down their bikes just to store them," Thomas answers my unspoken question. "But the real serious types keep them in these specialized cases."

Now that I look at them, I realize the design mimics the shape of a bike with the front wheel removed for storage. Behind them is a larger cardboard box with a simple image of a bike drawn on the side.

I flip through the passenger list, scanning for each indication of someone traveling with a bike. I count the notations, then the boxes, then the notations again.

"There are too many boxes," I say.

"Too many?" Sam echoes me.

"Yes. Sam, I have to go, I need my hands."

"Emma, don't hang up. I need to know what's going on," he argues.

"I'll call you back."

The phone goes into my pocket, and my mind focuses completely on the discrepancy.

"Look," I tell Thomas. "There is one more box over there than checked bikes. Can someone get a bike on board without it being listed?"

"Everything is accounted for when it comes into the baggage room," he insists.

"I'm getting the feeling that isn't entirely accurate," I mutter.

Stuffing the papers back in my bag, I walk over to the bike boxes and examine them. Each has a tag indicating the owner. I'm about to take the passenger list out again to compare when my eyes fall on one to my side. I pick up the tag and look down at it.

Emma Griffin.

"I can assure you I didn't bring a bike with me," I tell Thomas. "I haven't even ridden a bike since I was a little girl. It's not something I'm eager to try again any time soon."

I kneel down in front of the box and find a padlock securing it closed.

"It would be fine if you did. You know what they say. You never forget how to ride a bike," Thomas comments, as if he's trying desperately to hang onto normal conversation while a murderer is possibly loose on his train.

"I tend to avoid trusting advice from a group of people who won't even give their name," I reply "This lock requires a combination..." I murmur.

I rest my forehead in my hand and stare at the lock for a beat before starting to spin the dial.

"What? What did you figure out?" Thomas asks.

"The card Sam found says Happy Sweet Sixteen. Maybe that's it. The date of my sixteenth birthday. Seven, twenty-three... the year I turned sixteen. That was... oh-seven."

I set the last digit in place and give the lock a yank. It doesn't budge. Adjusting the dial slightly to make sure they are perfectly aligned, I try again. It still won't move. I let out an exasperated sigh and drop down to sit on my heels. Nothing else comes to mind. And I'm increasingly aware of every second passing me by. I take out my phone and call Sam.

"This bike box has a tag with my name on it," I tell him. "But it has a lock on it that requires a combination. I tried my sixteenth birthday, but it didn't work."

"But that's the only thing that makes sense."

"I know. Why else would the clue be in a sweet sixteen card? That has to mean something. I highly doubt someone who would go to this much detail, forgot paper, and just used the first greeting card they found sitting around," I point out.

"Wait," Thomas says. "That's the year you turned sixteen, so you were born in ninety-one?"

"Yes," I say. "Why?"

"July twenty-third?"

I narrow my eyes at him. "Yes. My sixteenth birthday was July, twenty-third, two thousand and seven. Seven, twenty-three, zero-seven."

He seems to think about this for a moment, his confused expression twisting as he considers the lock.

"Why would you choose one digit off for your luggage?"

"What do you mean why…"

My heart sinks, and I reach up for the lock. I shift the number in the middle down one digit.

"I—I didn't mean to be nosy," Thomas stammers, sounding worried and embarrassed. "I just happened to see you put your combination in when I brought your luggage earlier. I didn't realize it was your birthday at the time, but just now it occurred to me it was a different number."

I pull on the lock, and it falls open. My breath catches in my throat.

"The twenty-second," I whisper.

CHAPTER THIRTY

ANSON

FIVE MONTHS AGO...

T he pencil made a smooth stroke across the paper, the edge of the ruler guiding it. Sharp and precise. He wouldn't settle for anything less. Not in anything, but especially not in this. It had to be precise. It had to be perfect. If it wasn't—if there was only one small thing the tiniest bit off—it could ruin everything. That thought almost made him laugh. Somehow the thought of ruining the destruction of a building and the mass murder of the people inside struck him as funny. It would only really be ruined if it was stopped, and he would be sure it wasn't.

A mistake with his drawings wouldn't stop the explosion. But it would change the impact. He was very specific in how he wanted this event to unfold. He knew the exact extent and power behind the device he created. It wasn't just thrown together or devised for maximum destruction. There was no point in that. Arbitrarily leveling an entire area was far more along the lines of what Lotan would plan. He had a love for the theatrical, for the massive scale that would send the biggest ripples across whatever calm pond he wanted to destroy.

There used to be a delicacy in what Lotan did. He had a fine touch, discipline. He could create terror with something so subtle it was barely noticeable, but to those who noticed, it was horrifying. Carefully timed accidents. Systematic vandalism. Threats that flowed in the undercurrent, sowing distrust that bred panic that bred death. It was magnificent.

Then, like so many other things, that careful, masterful touch slipped through his fingers. He no longer had the time to concentrate on those things. Lotan turned his attention instead to building his empire. Selling weapons. Arming soldiers. Providing defense and comfort to cartels. When he did have time for the mission, he was too distracted. He designed the big spectacles, the evening national news special fodder.

Their days of glory disappeared. He no longer cared about the grains of sand or the trough of the wave. Leviathan became only about the crest of foam.

It was all because of her, Anson knew it. Others might not have recognized what was happening. Some weren't privy to her existence at all. But as time went by, he learned more about her and how deeply she was buried under Lotan's skin. Anson believed it would get better. For a time, he told himself it was going to change. It had to change. Lotan's need to watch over her would eventually fade.

But it only grew. It was no longer just about watching. Soon enough, she was all he talked about, and Anson's devotion slipped. The more Lotan gave of himself to the useless endeavor, to the shadows and corpses, the more Anson questioned his worthiness as a leader. He did everything for Lotan. He followed him without question, served him without hesitation. He did everything asked of him and more. So many times when Lotan and the others watched the news or read the papers with pride in their eyes and the gleeful sound of mayhem pounding in their hearts, it was Anson's drawings, his plans, his observations that brought them there.

Yet, he was never acknowledged anymore. Not in so many years. All of Lotan's energy and attention had gone to her. And for what? She was smart. She showed skill. But was that enough? Was she truly as exceptional as Lotan seemed to think she was?

Even if she was, would the world collapse without her? Would everything just cease to be? Would there be nothing more to strive for because she wasn't in the world anymore?

Would that be the ultimate spectacle? The purest form of chaos?

Perhaps. And perhaps not.

But finally, it was for him to decide.

CHAPTER THIRTY-ONE

I take the lock off and pull the two halves of the plastic shell apart. I've only gotten it open a few inches when I know something is horribly wrong. Blood trickles out and pools on the floor. The farther I push the box open, the more comes out, until there's a shift and something solid tumbles out. It lands on the floor in front of me with a thud.

I stare down at a hand, severed at the wrist. Long bright red nails blend with the spreading blood on the floor, and a narrow gold band on one finger makes my stomach turn.

Thomas clamps his hand over his mouth and turns away. His shoulders shake, and his body heaves forward, but he manages to hold onto himself.

"Emma? Emma?" I hear Sam's voice. For a few seconds, I can't figure out where it's coming from. Then I realize I've dropped my phone. "Emma? What is that?"

I use the side of my hand to carefully push the phone across the floor away from the bike box. I know he can only see the ceiling of the baggage car right now, but I need to be as careful about this as I can.

"It's a body," I tell him. "A woman, as far as I can tell. She's been dismembered."

Thomas gags again. He waves in my direction and rushes out of the car. I want to lunge after him, to tell him he can't leave, but I don't. Whatever type of game this person's disturbed mind thinks we're playing, this is a crime scene. Not a joke. Not a prop. This is a human being butchered and stuffed in a box to be found like a demented Easter egg. As much as I worry about the conductor revealing this increasingly twisted chain of secrets and putting everyone at risk, I also have to think about the eventual end. When it's done and our attention turns to giving this woman her voice back. I can't let him contaminate the crime scene or distract me from the incredibly delicate process of examining it further.

"Take pictures of it and send them to me," Sam instructs. "Then delete them from your phone. I'm keeping an ongoing record of evidence to give to the police when this is over."

"Will it ever be over?" I ask.

"Of course it will."

There's strength in his voice, complete faith in me, but I know horror is rolling through his veins.

"I'm going to open the box a little further. I want to disturb the body as little as possible, but I need to make sure this is all we're dealing with," I tell him.

I don't put voice to the possibility that the bomb we've been hunting is nestled inside the box with the body. Positioning myself behind the case, I reach over it and ease the halves of the case open further, then walk around to look inside. From this angle, I can see legs in a pair of leggings, bent and folded up in an unnatural position. Behind them is the torso. My mind starts to spin as I stare at it, forcing myself to accept what I see. A blue sweater. And against the chest, where the head is stuffed with the face mercifully concealed, a lock of stained hair that was once blonde.

"It's the woman that man saw near my seat," I say. "Now I know why I wasn't able to find her when I came looking for her."

"Who is this guy?" he asks. "You said he was squirrely."

"I don't know anything about him. He wasn't sitting there when I got on the train, but he insisted he was there when I went to the snack car. When I went to ask him about seeing the woman, he asked what branch of law enforcement I was in."

"Why would he ask that?" Sam asks.

"He told me he's a private investigator, and apparently, I have a tell."

"Did you tell him?"

"No. I asked him about the woman he saw. The woman who is in pieces at my feet."

"Emma, take pictures," Sam says.

I pick up my phone and snap a few images, deleting them as soon as I send them to Sam. Something catches my eye, and I lean down to get a better look. What I thought was one of her fingernails sticking up from behind her thigh isn't red. It's pink. The corner of a bright pink envelope.

"Sam, there's another envelope in with her. I'm going to get it," I tell him.

"Be careful."

I try to avoid touching her as much as I can as I reach in and take hold of the corner of the envelope. The side of my palm brushes against her leg. I suppress a shudder. She's still warm. So many people think of death as being instantly cold. As if the heart stops beating and the brain dies, and everything instantly goes away. Perhaps there's wisps of the concept of the soul in there. It's easier to think of a human being as warm and vibrant when it encapsulates the soul. And as soon as that soul is gone, they like to believe it takes all warmth with it. All that's left is a cold hard shell.

It is never as clean and easy as that. I have no problem believing in a soul. But I know death is not as simple as it just sliding out like a gust of breath and leaving nothingness behind. There may be times when it can be like that. When the end of a life is quiet and gentle, and a body and soul release each other softly. But that has far from been my experience.

I have seen death rip the soul from the body, tearing it out and leaving the body gasping, clawing to find anything left.

Either way, it isn't a single instant. There is no definite second when the person is fully there and then another when it is fully gone. Life doesn't blink out like a light. It filters away like filling cupped hands with water. It's there, and then it's not, but not immediately. It slides away, a little at a time. The heart and the brain first, then the muscles and the organs. Skin and bones are last. These cells can live on in the dead for many days before they finally succumb.

It isn't lost on me that even though her body is tattered and broken, the part of her closest to my touch, the skin just beneath her clothes, is still alive.

The envelope is exactly the same as the one Sam found. I carry it several feet away from the bike box and pick up the phone to show him. He watches in silence as I open it and draw out the card.

"It's the same birthday card," he notes.

I nod and open it. The card is the same, but the message written inside is different.

"'Will there be another? New game. Catch me and maybe there won't be. Have you figured out my secret? Keeping looking, and I'll tell you. Are you watching the time? Watch yourself, Emma. Can't be long now. Are you feeling mixed up? Imagine how the lion and the eagle feel. It's not what it looks like. Hurry now. One stops, both do.'"

My mouth feels dry when I finish reading.

"There isn't another body," Sam comments. "At least that's something to be thankful for."

"This card has been in with her body for hours. He's not playing in real-time. Everything is already in motion. The only thing we can change is stopping that bomb from going off when this train gets to the station. And that starts with finding out why that man said he saw the woman in the blue sweater at my computer when he couldn't have."

"He couldn't have?"

My head snaps up in response to the voice, and I see Thomas standing at the door. He's pale, and the collar of his shirt is damp from where he's splashed water on his face. I shake my head.

"No. I don't know why he would tell me he saw her at my seat, but there is no way this woman could have been the one to get my computer out of my bag," I tell him carefully.

"Why not?" he asks.

"I touched her, Thomas. Her body is in full rigor mortis. She's been dead for more than three hours. More than likely, she came onto this train exactly like we found her."

CHAPTER THIRTY-TWO

"You need to keep that man exactly where he is," Sam tells me. "Until this train stops and we can get hands on him, he can't be left unattended."

"Sam, there's nothing I can do right now but check in on him. This train is forty-five minutes from getting to the station. That means I have less than an hour to figure out another of Dr. Suess-iopath's riddles before two trains worth of people die."

"What do you mean?" Thomas asks, and I realize we never told him the full extent of what we had to drag him into.

I take a step toward him, again trying to position myself as much as I can between him and the carnage. Again, trying to protect him.

"You remember I told you if we alerted outside law enforcement or train security, there would be dire consequences for everyone on both trains?"

He nods. "Yes."

"Sam and I believe whoever's doing this has hidden a bomb somewhere on one of the trains. If either of the trains stops for any reason before we find it, it will go off. The only problem is, the trains are almost an hour apart. An explosion on either train wouldn't fully destroy both trains. It would likely lead to a crash and possibly damage from debris."

"Why is that a problem?" Thomas asks.

"Because we don't know which train it is, and the note says if one stops, both do. Which means there could be more than one bomb, or he could have something else planned. Either way, we have to figure it out. There is so much more to this that I can't explain to you, and I can't take up more of the time I don't have to keep an eye on him. We're on a train. He can't go anywhere."

"Couldn't you arrest him? Or at least detain him?"

I shake my head. "First, there's nothing to arrest him for. Making strange comments isn't enough grounds to arrest someone for a double murder. Second, I don't have a pair of cuffs or zip ties handy. Even if I did, if I detained him without evidence, we couldn't hang onto him for too long. And even then, it might be too late.

"Emma, you're covered in blood," Sam points out. "You can't go out into the train like that."

I look down at myself. My hands are bloodied, and the cuffs of my sweatshirt are soaked.

"Come with me," Thomas says. I follow him out of the baggage car and into the bathroom in the sleeping car. "You clean up. I'll go to your suitcase and get you another shirt."

"Emma, I have to ask you something," Sam says once he leaves.

"What?" I ask, glancing over to where I've set my phone.

"How would someone know the combination to your luggage? When have you ever shared that with anyone?"

"What do you mean? No one knows the combination. Well, you and Thomas do now," I tell him.

"You must have told someone. How else would this guy know to use that as the combination to the lock?" Sam asks.

I turn off the water and let out a sigh as I dry my hands on a paper towel and toss it away.

"It's not that he knew the combination," I say. "He knows my birthday. He wrote the clue in a birthday card. That was the point, not my combination. My combination had my birth year, remember? Not the year I turned sixteen."

"But that doesn't make sense," Sam muses. "Your birthday is the twenty-third."

"It is," I nod, picking up my phone and looking at him through the screen. "But when I was really little, my father used to tell me the story of when I was born. I was born a few seconds after midnight, so they declared my birthday the twenty-third. But Dad always said since a good part of me was out on the twenty-second, that should be my birthday. When my mother told him that's not how it worked, he said then he was going to make sure at least my head got to celebrate its birthday the way it was supposed to. She thought it was ridiculous, but it was something special he and I did. On the twenty-second he would celebrate just my head, so instead of going out and doing something, we would read or watch a movie. He would give me a gift just for my head. Lip balm or hair supplies..."

"Or earrings?" Sam asks.

I nod slowly. "Yes. And if I have to venture a guess, I'm going to say that woman is missing a pair of silver earrings."

"Emma..."

"It was a really silly tradition, and I'm fairly certain he kept up with it mostly because of how weird Mama thought it was. But it ended up becoming something we really loved. He would joke and call it my 'real' birthday and say the twenty-third is just a formality. My eyes, brain, and heart were all out on the twenty-second, so I was here, according to him."

"I never knew that," he says.

"No one does, Sam. I've never told anybody about that. Especially after Mama died. It was something really special just for the two of us. Other than when we were in Sherwood, we didn't even celebrate on the twenty-third. But, again, that's not something I told anybody. The only person who would know about that is my father."

Thomas comes back, and I brush fiercely at tears that have appeared on my cheeks.

"Are you alright?" he asks.

"I'm—I'm fine," I say, taking the sweatshirt he hands out to me. "Thank you for getting this for me."

He nods. "I don't know if I can be of any help with what you found there, or if it would be more beneficial for me to continue on with my work to try to keep people away from this part of the train."

"You should do your work. I'll come find you if I need your help."

"I will keep my eye on Mr. Steele," he says.

"Mr. Steele?" I raise an eyebrow.

"The man sitting a few rows behind you," he explains. "I thought you knew his name."

"No. He never introduced himself. Dean Steele?"

"Yes."

"Has he been on the train many times before?" I ask.

Thomas shrugs. "Honestly, I can't tell you. I don't remember him. His name just stuck with me when I looked at his ticket."

I nod. "Me, too."

He walks away, and I sit down on the floor, pulling out my computer.

"What are you doing?" Sam asks.

"I'm staying here for as long as I can to try to keep people out of the baggage car."

"Read the clue to me again," he says.

I read him the card.

"A new game. So, not hide and seek, anymore. I'm not sure I believe that considering this bomb is still hidden," I say.

"But there's a new game to figure out what to do next. Only this time, he doesn't tell us which one."

"'Catch me.' That's what he keeps saying. And he mentions the time again. But this end part. The lion and the eagle. That's something. That's a message," I point out.

"A symbol of some kind? The train cars don't have symbols or mascots or anything. Maybe an organization?" Sam asks.

"Wait. Sam. A lion and an eagle. A griffin. My name. It asks if I'm feeling mixed up, then mentions the lion and eagle."

"That next part, it's not what it looks like. Isn't a griffin exactly what it looks like? A lion and an eagle?"

"No," I murmur, shaking my head as I continue to stare at the note. "That's the point. It's not. It looks like someone took an eagle's head and attached it to a lion's body, but that's not what it is. In mythology, it's actually its own creature. It's something totally separate."

"The woman? We thought she could have something to do with this, so it looked like her, but it wasn't?" Sam suggests.

"No. I don't think it means 'look' that way. These notes have been telling us to look for something this whole time. Keep looking. It's talking about something tangible. Something with the appearance of something it's not." I read the note again, breaking it down into its parts, the sections that go together, and the ones that stand apart. "It uses the word 'watch' twice. Are you watching the time, and watch yourself."

Snippets of conversations and flashes of images go through my head. Little bits of moments that don't seem to have anything to do with each other but have now suddenly converged. I draw in a breath.

"Emma? What is it?" Sam asks.

"I think I have an idea."

CHAPTER THIRTY-THREE

ANSON

FIVE MONTHS AGO...

Anson's room was taken over by sketches and plans. Every time he finished one, his fingers itched to start the next. He told himself to take his time, to slow down, and go one step at a time. He had to build, to climb on the shoulders of one to get to the next. But he was too excited. For the first time in longer than he could remember, he felt alive.

It was a strange sensation, feeling life flowing through his veins and waking up every part of him when he hadn't even realized he was dead.

He had become exactly what Lotan wanted from him. That was a hard lesson. To go from thinking he mattered and was an important part of the mission, to knowing he was nothing but flesh and brain signals. Lotan didn't choose his followers lightly. He wasn't the type of man who assigned value to devotion in whatever form he could find it. There were plenty who would fall at his feet and do anything he said, simply by merit of the power of his speech. He could weave words and manipulate thoughts in a way unrivaled by anyone Anson ever met. Anyone he had even heard of.

But Lotan didn't just want worshipers to line his floor. He was looking for only the best. He wanted those who would believe what he believed, follow what he followed. As great and as extensive as his influence could be, the one humility about him was that he acknowledged he was just one man. What Lotan was capable of doing was tremendous on his own. But if he could find those who understood what he wanted, and could offer skills and intelligence, he could do so much more.

It took time for Anson to recognize it, but he eventually realized everyone who became a part of Leviathan went through the same process. They began as individuals. Lotan charmed them and showed them appreciation. He emphasized the very features he chose them for and ensured they knew he saw them. He looked right into their eyes. He spoke their names.

Over time, that faded. The details of them as individual people begin to fade away. They were broken down to their base elements so they could be used as tools. One by one, they gave up the details of themselves, the quirks and bits that made them into who they were.

For some of them, it was easy to overlook the sacrifice. They did not even realize what was actually happening. Because to them, they weren't giving those pieces of themselves up. They weren't losing them. For every piece of themselves, every detail, every memory, every trait they offered up to the Leviathan, the tattoo on their back, became more complex. Rather than defining themselves as who they were within, they displayed their worth on their skin.

That would always be with Anson. But he wanted more than the ink. More than the prestige and rank. He wanted to claim back what was taken. He wanted to understand Lotan's attachment to a woman far from his grasp. He wanted to prove even the mighty Lotan wasn't safe from chaos.

This is how it would start. A simple plan, but one that wouldn't soon be forgotten. And from there, another. Lotan was so used to being the one in control he wouldn't recognize when that was being drawn out from under him, little by little, like the tide washing away a sandcastle until there was no choice left but to watch it fall.

CHAPTER THIRTY-FOUR

LAMB

He hadn't heard anything from Finn in weeks. Not that he expected frequent contact. That would be far too dangerous. Any time he was able to communicate with him at all, it was dangerous. Either of them could get caught, and the consequences would be unimaginable. Lamb just had to wait patiently. He had to embody the name given to him. As much as he despised it, he embraced it as well. It reminded him of all that happened. How he got here. It wouldn't let him forget. Every time he heard it, it was just another chance for him to feel the disdain, to remember what this man thought of him.

Lotan used it as a way to break Lamb down. That's one of the many ways he had gotten into the minds of his followers. What at first seemed like a gesture of kindness—like a gift—became a weapon. Became a means of control. He had already watched so many of them fall. One by one, they let themselves get tangled and twisted into being a part of his thoughts. They were no longer their own. They were no longer the people they were before they met him and fell into line. They were a moving, breathing creature. A single writhing mass. A leviathan, under his control.

It was masterful to watch. The switch wasn't sudden. Often it was so gradual and subtle the person being dragged down into the darkness didn't even know what was happening. It was like a person stuck in a room filled with nitrogen gas. They craved Lotan's attention, like the body craves oxygen. They sought it out, clawed for it, tried to sip it from his breaths, his words, a fleeting glance. But it was never actually there. Their minds twisted these small moments to seem like they were still being acknowledged, still being honored. Just like every cell of the body will take in nitrogen and pretend it's oxygen.

It couldn't last forever. They were suffocating. Drowning. Yet they continued to try desperately. They worked harder. Devoted themselves more deeply. They dug down inside themselves to find anything that was left and give it over to him. Just like a person gasping in their final moments, they still believed they could find in him what they needed.

Lamb didn't tumble into that. He wouldn't let himself. There were moments when he almost did. He wasn't going to lie and pretend he always maintained absolute control. That wasn't realistic. Lotan's entire existence in his life was a matter of falling under his control, if only for a minute. He gulped the false air. He let himself slip under. But every time, just before drowning, he broke through the surface and found air. In the end, he knew something about Lotan no one else did. Something he didn't even know himself. And that's what kept Lamb's head above the water.

What happened now was for Emma. If he could figure a way out, he would go, but the chances of that happening were getting slimmer by the day. Ever since Finn left, Lotan's visits had become more frequent. He didn't just leave him there in the dark as he had before. There were times when he cast Lamb into a room and left him there with no light. No sound. He had no idea whether it was day or night or how much time had passed. He never explained it or even acknowledged it happened. There would just come a time when the door would open, light would sear into his eyes, and he would go back to his room.

Not anymore. Now Lotan came nearly every day. Some days, more than once. Sometimes he would ramble and rant, asking questions and demanding answers Lamb didn't have to give him, then spilling out the rage and frustration inside him. Sometimes he spoke calmly and quietly, almost like he didn't even realize Lamb was there. He spoke about the past; he dreamed of the future. Sometimes, he did nothing at all. He came in and sat, not moving, completely silent. Hours might pass with the almost tangible silence between them; then, he would simply get up and leave.

Lamb was watching him unravel. Something was happening. Something was chipping away at him. It was a tenuous time. At any moment, he could shatter, his life and empire flailing into tiny bits. Lamb could only hope the work was done by then, and that he would not be caught by the shrapnel.

CHAPTER THIRTY-FIVE

"The word 'watching' isn't accidental. He knows. He knows what I've been doing, but it's exactly what he wants me to be doing," I say.

"What are you talking about?" Sam asks.

I open my computer and pull up the vlog.

"Eric has been trying to get access to Mary Preston's private messages so we can find out what she was talking about with this See-at-Sea person. But since that might take a little bit of time, Bellamy looked at the profile for me. She wasn't able to put a whole lot of time into it, but she gave me some really interesting insights. A lot of it went along with my first instincts. The name was odd and didn't make a lot of sense, but she looked at the profile and saw things in it that I didn't. She said it didn't look like it was supposed to."

"What do you mean?"

"According to her, that type of name sounds much more like a young woman who's trying to be artistic or creative. But the way the pictures are laid out on a profile itself, it looks like a man made it. It's not artfully curated enough to be a photographer's page, and it's not a personal page either. It's not what it looks like."

"So, is that what the note's talking about?" Sam asks.

"Maybe, but I think it's more than that." I click on the name, but instead of the profile opening, a text box appears on the screen. "Wait, hold on. Something's changed." I show him the screen.

"Has that ever happened before?" he asks.

"No. I've never seen anything like that. It wants a password." I look at the fine print under the open box. "One guess."

"What's your guess?" Sam asks.

"I have an idea, but I don't want to risk it. If he says one guess, that's what he means. I don't want to tempt him. but I think I know how to figure it out."

"How?"

I dig through my bag for my pad of paper and pen. Turning the paper to the side, I write out the screen name in large block letters so I can see each individually.

"It isn't just the profile that isn't what it looks like. It's the name itself. When he references to the lion and the eagle in the note, it was talking about my name. My name is something that isn't what it seems to be. So, maybe this name is too."

"What does it mean?" Sam asks.

"It's not what it looks like," I whisper to myself. "It's not what it looks like."

I touch my pen to the paper. I try to look at them differently, to understand what it could be that it doesn't look like. My hand shakes slightly as the realization forms in my mind.

"It's not words," I tell him. "The name looks like it's made out of words. But it's not. It's letters."

"I don't understand."

I draw a line down from each of the segments, reading it out to him as I do it.

"See, at, sea. C-a-t-c. He, me. H, em, e. H, m, e." My pen digs so hard into the paper it almost tears through as I write out the words. "Catch Me."

CHAPTER THIRTY-SIX

ANSON

FOUR MONTHS AGO ...

Anson always hated the types of plans that didn't fall into place until the very last minute. He wanted things laid out in front of him, perfect and exact. He wanted to be able to envision every single moment and know the final outcome before it even began. He liked to watch the seconds fall like dominoes.

That wasn't the way this was. He had everything in place. His drawings had come to life. His sketches were now metal and powder. The final piece, the key that would make it all come together, wasn't there yet. He was confident it would be. He had been working for so long, doing everything he could to make it all work together. A little bit at a time. Cautious and strategic. At any point, it could have gone off the rails. But he controlled it. He continued until he could infiltrate not just her thoughts, but her very being. In a way, he became Lotan in those moments. He knew what it felt like.

But this woman would never be like Emma. She would never become his thoughts, his breath, his delusions. She was what she was, and soon she would be nothing. And yet, she would be everything. She would be exactly what she always wanted to be. Famous. Known.

Maybe not in the way she ever expected. Maybe not in the way she ever wanted. But few ever got exactly what they wanted. Perhaps this was more than she ever could have expected.

The world would know her name. They would know her face and the sound of her voice. They would flock to her image and join the masses who mourned for an image. A concept. That wasn't wrong. Not really, anyway. People needed something to hold on to, something to identify with. They wanted to feel like they were part of something, even when that was grief and loss. It made them feel stronger. Like they had collectively overcome something they barely even experienced.

But in order for that to happen, she needed to agree. She needed to say the words Anson had been waiting to hear.

"This was my plan."

It wasn't something she ever would have come up with on her own, but he needed her to believe she did. He needed her to take his suggestion and fuse it to her own thoughts so much she believed she had come up with it completely on her own. That would control her words. It would filter out any reference to him. When she spoke, she needed to speak about herself and only herself. After all, that's what they were all waiting for.

It was only hours now. Hours before he would know if his plan was going to work the way he hoped. There was a sick feeling in the waiting, but also strange exhilaration. A rush, like that moment at the top of the hill on a roller coaster.

The car pauses, and you dangle, listening to the click of the brakes, waiting for the drop.

CHAPTER THIRTY-SEVEN

IAN

SEVENTEEN YEARS AGO...

"Do you really have to leave?" he asked, pulling his wife into his arms.

She smiled at him. That was a smile he could never get enough of. From the first time he saw it, it took hold of him and wouldn't let go. He never wanted it to. She had given that smile to their daughter. It wasn't all the way there yet. She was still too young. There wasn't enough in her yet to form a smile like that. But it would be there someday. The time would come when she would have someone to look at who would bring that smile to her face and it would become everything.

For now, Ian was more than happy to have their daughter at home. She was still young. He could still protect her. It wouldn't be much longer before she was old enough to want to take on the world by herself, and he wouldn't be able to shield her. Her entire life, all he had ever tried to do was shield her. She would understand that one day. At least, he hoped she would.

"Yes, love. You know I do," Mariya said, looping her slim, graceful arms around his neck. "She needs me."

"I know she does," he sighed, letting his body rest against hers. He loved the way their breaths felt moving in and out together. "Have I told you recently how incredible you are?"

Mariya grinned and touched her soft mouth to his. There was a secret in that kiss. Something she only shared with him. So many, her whole life, had thought they shared her. They felt ownership over her because of what she did. She was willing to give them that comfort, to let them feel protected and reassured by the idea of her presence. After all, that's what she was there for. It's what she always wanted to do.

Even from her days up on the stage, the lights and the applause only filled her so much. She always said they felt like they were for somebody else. Like somehow, the scale and beauty meant for somebody else ended up in her. She used them as much to her advantage as she could, helping her family more than they could have ever imagined. But entertaining people wasn't right for her. She didn't want to be owned or shared by fans or bureaucrats. She just wanted her own life. Her own family.

Ian marveled at her bravery. For some, it would be hard to look at a woman of such delicate beauty, who moved with the elegance and grace of the stage even many years after she walked away and think of her as brave. But Mariya was the most courageous person he had ever known.

When others looked at her, they didn't see what she had gone through. They didn't see the fear she carried in her heart that night when she walked out onto the stage into her last spotlight. When she very first told him about it, she told him her shoes felt tight. He never really understood what that meant. But one day, after many years, she brought her old ballet shoes out of the box where she'd shoved them away and showed them to him.

From a distance, they would look beautiful, just like her. But close up, he could see the pink satin cutaway at the tip of the toe to make it less slippery. The dust and dirt darkening the sides. The frays at the end of the ribbons. Streaks of blood inside.

She was never going to have to wear them again after that night.

That's what she told herself. Of course, nobody else knew that. The rest of the company planned on three more shows before going back to Russia. Then it would be another season, another production. But not for her. Her final bow that night was truly her final bow.

Now, many years later, Ian knew she looked back on that like a different life. It was like somebody else had lived all that. She was finally doing exactly what she was meant to do. It was no longer about entertaining people but helping them. And she did. Countless people. They lived because of her.

"I won't be gone long. Then, Easter," she said happily.

"Did you kiss Emma good night?" he asked.

"Yes. Of course I did. When she wakes up in the morning, make her pancakes. I left cookie cutters on the counter so you can make them into the shapes of flowers for her. She can help you boil some eggs so they can be in the refrigerator for Sunday."

"Do you think you'll be able to call?" he asked.

"I don't know, darling. I will if I can," she told him.

"Don't, if it's too dangerous. You know we'll be here."

"I know you will. I love you," she said.

"I love you, too," he told her.

He brought her close and kissed her. There were only a few moments left before she had to leave, and he wasn't going to waste any of them.

"I'll see you soon," she whispered.

He walked her out to the car and kissed her one last time through the window.

"Do you have everything you need?" he asked.

"I think so. Goodbye, my love."

CHAPTER THIRTY-EIGHT

NOW

I type the words into the box and watch it dissolve away to reveal the profile. A breath I didn't even realize I was still holding in my lungs rushes out of me in relief. But I know I can't let myself relax. That was just one piece. Just the beginning. There is so much more, and the minutes are running thin.

"What's next?" Sam asks. "Is there anything new? New pictures, anything?"

I scroll to the bottom of the page, past the pictures of the ocean and the sand I've already looked at countless times before. On the very bottom row are three new images. I notice a little icon in the corners.

"These are videos," I tell him.

"So, watch them," he says.

I start to click on the first but hesitate.

"Wait. What if is this is like the password. What if I'm not supposed to watch all of them, but only the right one. One guess, remember?"

"Which one, then?" Sam asks.

I look at each of the three images, each showing a screenshot from the video. The first is a road and in the corner, it looks like a leg and foot, like someone is walking. The second is a picture of me jogging down the sidewalk in my neighborhood in Sherwood.

The third takes the breath out of every inch of my being. I've never seen this picture of my mother smiling back at me. She's looking over her shoulder, her hair tumbling down longer than I ever saw it. There's a glint in her eye, a laugh. I want to click on that one. I long to hear her voice. To see her move again.

But I have to stop myself. I remember what the note said.

"This one," I tell him, pointing to the second video. "The note says watch yourself. For once, he was being literal." I click on the image and see the time at the bottom. "This video is two hours long," I lament.

"We don't even have a fraction of that time," he sighs.

"What are we supposed to do? How are we supposed to know what part of the video is going to help us? The beginning? The end?" I ask, my anxiety ratcheting up.

For every second that passes by, my breath becomes a little shallower, and my veins seem to constrict a little more.

"Emma," Sam suddenly starts. "The card. It was the same card as the first one. Happy Sweet Sixteen. It has something to do with your birthday."

I look at the time stamp again. Clicking on the cursor, I drag it slightly and reveal an account of the hours, minutes, seconds, and fractions of seconds. Moving carefully, I drag it over until the numbers correspond to the date of my sixteenth birthday. Zero hours. Seven minutes. Twenty-three seconds. Seven milliseconds. I pause, then pull it back to twenty-two seconds. My stomach hurts doing it. I can't let myself think about it too much. I can't let my thoughts go down the path they want to follow, the logical progression that makes me want to scream.

"Are you ready?" I ask.

"Go ahead," he says.

I click play.

CHAPTER THIRTY-NINE

ANSON

Maybe one day, when all this was over, and they rebuilt, Anson would offer his services. They would rebuild, of course. It's what they did. What the city prided itself on. They would panic first, mourn second. Then would come rage, then resilience. They would clear away the ground and build again. And Anson could go to them and offer his expertise.

He could explain to them why the security cameras they had in place were woefully insufficient. He could show them the blind spots and the entire swaths of area around the building that went completely uncovered. He would show them how easy it was for someone to move across the parking lot in just the right places and slip close to the building. He would show them how if somebody really wanted to, if they really had motivation, they could overcome the simplistic locks and walk right inside.

The security system looked impressive from the outside. At least, to anyone who didn't really know what they were looking at. They saw a keypad and a screen requiring a code. He saw a game. And not a difficult one to win at that. But they would find that out eventually.

He'd be happy to tell them and to offer to create a much more effective approach. When the new building was built. When this one was gone.

For now, he walked through the dusty, sticky air of the back room. Nobody knew he was there, and they never would. He wasn't going to be there for long. All he needed to do was find access to the ventilation system. Then it was just a matter of setting a timer, activating a trigger, and walking away.

Part of him wished he had made a second of the boxes he set into place. He knew what it was meant to do. And that was as good as knowing what it was going to do. He never designed anything that didn't work exactly the way he thought it would. He could see the pieces in his mind; know exactly how they were going to interact and what they were going to do. That's what made him what he was.

But he still wanted to see it happen. He wanted to have the chance to watch the metal split and the smaller metal creatures inside emerge. That's what would leave them guessing. Eventually, there would be an investigation. Remember, this wasn't designed for annihilation. Just destruction. The area would swarm, and everybody would have ideas of what happened. Of who did it. Accusations would fly. Tentative bonds would shatter. And someone would try to figure out exactly how it happened.

They never would. They would never be able to understand exactly how the explosion happened the way it did to create the exact damage it was going to create. But that was part of the fun. The guesses would just keep coming. Every one of them was a tiny seed of chaos. It would never let them rest.

Anson got out of the station and crossed the parking lot to the small patch of grass and trees that separated it from a gas station on the corner. He waited there, watching the door. A white car drove into the lot and parked. There she was. Already holding her phone when she climbed out of the car. She struggled to pull her suitcase out of the trunk. He waited until she turned off her phone before he strode toward her, his long legs eating up the pavement, so he got to her in seconds. Big hands easily got the bag out of place, and she turned to smile at him.

"Thanks," she said.

There wasn't even the flicker of recognition in her eyes. There wouldn't be. She'd never seen his face.

"No problem. Where are you headed?" he asked.

She set the bag down and pulled the handle so she could swing it around behind her.

"Baltimore," she told him. "Just a quick trip."

Anson nodded. "Sounds like fun. You should check out the Harbor."

She smiled. "I've heard that before. I guess I'll have to take the recommendation."

A black car slid into the parking lot and moved around to the side. It didn't matter if they saw him. They didn't know if he was meant to be there or not, and they would never question it.

"Have a good time on your trip," he said, starting away from her.

Behind him, her phone made a cheerful chirp, alerting her to a message she wouldn't know was scheduled hours before. *Did you get to the station alright? Your ticket is waiting at the window. I'll be watching!*

She glanced down at it and smiled, then typed a fast response. The alert in his pocket was silent, but he'd read it later.

"Thank you again..." she called after him, her voice trailing in that way that was supposed to suggest a pause, an empty space in her sentence it was his responsibility to fill.

"Anson."

She smiled.

"Anson. I'm Mary."

CHAPTER FORTY

HIM

SEVENTEEN YEARS AGO...

I t didn't matter how far they went.
It didn't matter where they tried to hide.
He would find them.

Nothing could protect them. Not now. Not ever. They might have run, but he would chase them. They might have hidden themselves away, but he would find them. They were lost without him. They were far more lost with him. In the end, it wouldn't matter.

Let them run. He had no need to go after them yet. They weren't going to get away. It didn't matter how much time passed, they would always be in the palm of his hand, even if they didn't know it. For now, he would mourn. Let them run. The longer they did, the more their fear would take over. Their bodies would weaken; their hearts wouldn't sustain them.

The fear wouldn't be worse than him. Nothing for them would ever be worse than him. For the rest of their lives, no matter what they faced, no matter what choices they made, he would haunt them. He would be the horror they faced when they closed their eyes at night. He would be what kept their lights on and made their hands shake.

That fear would be a constant, gnawing reminder that ate at them and dissolved them from the inside. It would add to the torment. Create another layer to the pain he would cause them. But it would never be worse than him.

They knew that.

So he decided to let them run. He would let them fill their skin with ink to cover themselves. He would let them slide on their bellies through the swamps. He would even let them breathe. He would even let them laugh. That laughter would open them up to more of the fear, like prying their jaws open to pour in the poison.

That night, he didn't know where they were. They didn't meet him in the designated spot. He couldn't reach them. But he would find them. The day would come when he would find them, and they would pay for what they did.

It would never be enough. Both of them combined weren't worth the life they took. But he would ensure they gave every last drop of what they could to atone for Mariya.

CHAPTER FORTY-ONE

NOW

There's blood on my shoes. I know it's there, and I'm tracking it along the carpet, but I can't stop. I can't do anything about it. In my mind, I imagine the fibers absorbing it. No matter how hard they try to clean it, it'll never go away. The memories will never go away.

I burst into the first empty train car on the way back to mine just in time to see the sliding door in front of me open. Intense blue eyes stare at me through the afternoon sunlight coming through the windows. I stop in the middle of the aisle, my hand going to my gun.

"What are you doing?" I ask. "You shouldn't be back here."

"Neither should you," he says.

"I don't believe I asked your permission."

"And I didn't ask yours. But I will ask you to get your hand away from your firearm. I'm not exactly a fan of being in a closed space with a gun when I'm unarmed," he says.

"You need to start talking," I say. "Or you are going to have a whole lot more to worry about than my hand on my gun."

"What are you talking about?"

"Why did you tell me you saw a blonde woman in a blue sweater at my seat?"

"Because you asked me if I saw anybody," he replies, confused.

"I know for a fact you didn't see her, so try again. Why did you say you saw that woman at my seat?"

"What do you mean you know for a fact I didn't see her?" he asks. "What's going on?"

"You asked me earlier what branch of law enforcement I'm in. I'm FBI. And right now, you've found yourself in the middle of a murder investigation, so I suggest you take your attitude down a few notches and start answering questions. Starting with why you lied about her being at my seat," I say.

"Murder?" he asks.

I don't have the luxury of being subtle anymore. Seconds are ticking away. Everyone is going to know about the bodies soon enough, and I would rather it be because I told them and was able to stop a tragedy, then because they all joined them.

"The woman you described as being the person who took my computer out of its bag is dead. She's been dead since long before you supposedly saw her. If I don't miss my guess, she never stepped foot on this train alive. So how is it that you could possibly describe her down to the color of her sweater?" I ask.

He swallows hard.

"I saw her on the platform," he tells me. "When I was walking to the train, I happened to notice her. She stood out because everybody else was already on the train, and she was just standing there, talking to one of the employees. I thought she was..." his voice trails off for a second before he rebounds. "Later, when you asked me if I saw anybody at your seat, I panicked and described the first person who came to mind. I thought it would make sense. I didn't think anything of seeing her because you looked similar."

"Why would it matter?" I ask. Some private investigator.

"Because I knew if I didn't have someone to describe, you would know I hadn't been sitting in that seat the entire time," he says.

"Look, I don't have time for this bullshit. You can explain to the sheriff later why it mattered so much for me to think you were sitting there. There's something else I need to know," I tell him. "Your name is Dean Steele."

He straightens, his shoulders squaring off slightly.

"Yes."

"Tell me, Dean. What do you know about Mary Preston?"

CHAPTER FORTY-TWO

ANSON

FOUR MONTHS AGO...

Anson watched from Mary's perspective as she scanned the bus station, taking in the monotony of just another day. People shuffled around, getting ready for their trips. Some had just gotten off of buses and were going about the motions of assimilating to being at the end of the journey. That was one of the more interesting things he had observed about some people traveling. Even if it was a very short trip, there was still a sense of permanence about the travel itself. Whether they were in a car or a bus or a train or a plane, somehow, that became reality. It felt like it was going to last forever. But then it ended, and they had to go through the process of getting used to something else all over again.

Those are the types of people who wanted to change clothes immediately or who put on makeup before stepping off their chosen mode of transportation. They would walk a few steps from the gate, put their luggage down, and brush off their clothes. Or dig through their purses like they thought something might have changed between the time they were sitting and now.

But then there were the others who barely even seemed to notice they had traveled at all. It was just one step to another. A constant flow of their life, unbroken by any change of pace. Those are the types of people who made a straight line from the gate to the door without hesitation. Didn't pause, didn't stop to look around at their surroundings or anyone else. They didn't have luggage to pick up or clothes to adjust. They were just ready.

The slow movement of her camera allowed Anson to take in all the types of people. This wasn't the first time Mary had done a live stream of one of her adventures, but this one was different. Instead of broadcasting it out to all of her followers, the live portion was just for him. Because he had been the one to recommend her trip to Baltimore. Because he had guided her into thinking the journey was her own idea. He told her he wanted to go along for the ride with her, that she could post the video later, but he wanted to be the first one to experience it with her.

She was happy to comply, and it brought him right into the epicenter of all he had been thinking about for weeks. She turned toward the door, and he got to see her perspective of Greg walking in. The way she paused told Anson she noticed him, too. He walked through the doors with absolute purpose. His eyes didn't move from in front of him as he walked toward the back of the station. She couldn't see it, but he knew his other hand tightly gripped the handle of a dark green duffel bag hanging down by his side.

Anson didn't know what was inside the bag. That part of this mission wasn't shared with him. He only knew Greg would be here, and for how long. It was why he chose this place and this day. It was why he went in search of Mary.

The camera stopped recording Greg as Mary went to the counter. He watched the edges of the screen, timed the steps he'd measured out in his drawings. Greg would have put the bag in the locker by now. It was time for him to walk back out of the station and get in the car still waiting for him. The security cameras in the station would capture Greg making his way through the crowd but lose him when he got to the lockers. Mary's stream would give the human touch people craved, the brutality and tragedy news watchers said disgusted them, but was the whole reason they watched.

And everyone would know her name.

Just as he expected her to, Mary started for the information desk on the far side of the bus station. One of her habits was to get a luggage tag every time she traveled. He highly doubted any of them were discernible from the others with the exception of what she wrote on them, but it held meaning for her. What he didn't expect was for her to step into line behind Greg.

He wasn't supposed to be at the information desk. His prescribed path was into the station, to the lockers, and back out. Yet, there he was, standing in line waiting for the man behind the desk to be free. Mary lifted her camera high to record herself talking about her luggage tag, and Anson caught Greg sliding something across the desk.

"Give this to Emma Griffin," he said.

Anson's mouth curled into a smile and laughed. He'd underestimated Greg. He never would have thought he would defy Lotan. But it only worked in his favor. Greg didn't know it, but he had just handed Emma right into his grip.

Mary got her tag and walked over to a seat where she would wait. Buzzing with anticipation, his excitement even greater now, Anson waited. Time slipped by. Second after second. The hum of the passengers in the bus station seemed to get louder and louder as it got closer. His hand tightened around the rough stone corner of the convenience store where he had positioned himself. He wanted to be far enough away not to catch any of the debris, but close enough to feel the rumble.

His hands trembled. He took a breath and let out a roar as the explosion tore the air around him.

CHAPTER FORTY-THREE

GREG

They were waiting for him. Not just the ones in the car who brought him to the station and were going to drive him away when it was over. There were more. He saw Fisher in the parking lot, talking to a woman who seemed excited about whatever trip she was about to take. He didn't pay any attention to the car as it drove into the parking lot, but that didn't mean he didn't notice it.

Greg walked directly inside, his hand gripping the duffel bag tightly at his side. It felt strangely heavy, for having so little in it. Not that he was allowed to see what was inside. That wasn't part of his clearance. He had to trust that what Lotan needed was what was right. He had his guesses of what it could be. A bus station made an ideal drop-off point, even with the occasional police officer roaming through like there was here. The lack of metal detectors that had become ubiquitous in other places made it easier to move things in and out. Passengers were scanned before they got on the buses, but there was nothing screening anyone just walking through. It was very easy for someone to leave something in a locker and for another person to come pick it up. Just that smoothly. No one questioned a person walking through a bus station with a bag.

He paid close attention to what was happening around him. He watched the doors. He looked at each face. Fisher never followed him inside. No one around him looked familiar. The risk was still there, but it was worth taking. He slid the folded piece of paper from his pocket and handed it to the man at the information desk.

"Give this to Emma Griffin," he said.

It might not get to her. There was no guarantee she would pass through here. But he hoped she would. If Finn did what he needed to do, she would. He just needed to get her there.

It seemed like a longshot. But there was nothing more he could do.

Following the exact path given to him when he was given the job, Greg walked across the lobby and toward the glass doors. He caught another glimpse of the woman who was with Fisher in the parking lot, sitting in one of the plastic chairs as she waited. She was invested in her phone, lost in something on the screen.

Just as he expected, the black car was already sitting in front of the station when he stepped outside. Then heat sank through his clothes and into his back as bits of debris blasting through the air cut into his skin. He didn't know what happened. He laid there for a minute, feeling nothing but shock and surprise when hands grabbed him and dragged him into the waiting car.

He slid across the seat, and the man in the driver's seat glared through the rearview mirror at him.

"What took you so long?" he asked.

"There were people watching," Greg lied.

The driver shoved his foot on the gas, causing the car to lurch forward. A bus was blocking the way out of the parking lot, so he whipped around the side of the building. Greg turned his head toward the glare of the sunlight reflecting off the shattered glass and twisted metal of the doors that were destroyed by a ball of flame.

CHAPTER FORTY-FOUR

NOW

D ean's face goes pale, but before he says anything, the door opens again, and Thomas rushes through. I shove past Dean to him.

"Thomas, I need to get into one of the sleeper cars," I tell him.

"The sleeper cars?" he asks.

"The last clue was a video of me. In it was a clip of an interview I did about my case in Feathered Nest. In it, I say that place forced me to face the darkest parts of my life. That's where it is. I need to get into sleeper car thirteen," I tell him. "The passenger must be in there, but I can't get inside. Can you find the attendant for me?"

Thomas shakes his head.

"There is no passenger in the sleeper cars," he tells me.

"Of course there is. I saw him get on board this morning. Then Sam called while we were still waiting to leave the station and told me the information that he got from the station. The man staying in the sleeper car got off the train to smoke a cigarette, but he didn't bring his ticket or his ID with him, so he was having trouble getting back on. But it got resolved, and we left."

Thomas shakes his head again. "No. That's the thing. There was a man in the sleeper car on this train. He got off and didn't have his ticket or his ID to get back on. Our supervisor called Miranda, the attendant of the sleeper car, to tell her there was a passenger having an issue who needed her assistance. He asked her to go into the cabin and get his ID and ticket for him. And she did get his ID but forgot his ticket. The passenger got impatient waiting for her to come back and walked away. Eventually, they decided to go ahead and leave." He draws in a breath as if trying not to cry. "And now I can't find Miranda."

"It's taken this long for you to notice the attendant who was supposed to be taking care of a non-existent passenger hasn't been seen?" I ask.

Thomas shakes his head. "Emma..."

"I have twenty minutes, Thomas."

"I knew where she was supposed to be. With Mr. Jones."

The confession strikes me silent.

"Excuse me, what?" I finally ask.

"They've been having an affair for six months. He schedules his trips to Georgia for when Miranda is working as an attendant for the sleeper cars. But he gets a regular seat, so he doesn't cause suspicion. Right after the tickets are checked, he goes to be with her. Usually, he comes back a few times during the ride, but when we got confirmation the passenger in the sleeper car wasn't going to be on board, I assumed they were going to spend the entire ride together."

"You knew this? We've been searching the train for bodies, and you never thought it was important to tell me the passenger you swore up and down wasn't missing, actually was? Along with your coworker?" I ask incredulously.

"I didn't think they were missing. I just told you, I thought they were together. I saw her at the beginning of the day, and I heard from her after the incident with the passenger. I thought everything was fine," he says.

"You heard from her?" I ask. "What do you mean you heard from her?"

"She radioed in to tell us she got the message about the passenger and handled it."

"Handled it?" I ask. "Thomas, I need you to call the other train and find out if that passenger got on board. And find out what car he was supposed to be in on this train."

"Number twenty-seven," he tells me.

I nod and look at Dean. "You need to go back to your seat and not say anything to anyone."

"Why can't I come with you?" he asks.

"You are not a part of this."

"I'm a private investigator. I can help," he argues.

"I don't need your help. I'm not involving another civilian in this. Right now, I'm still not sure I fully believe your story, and I need to discuss your involvement with Mary Preston. You need to go back to your seat and stay there until you've been interviewed."

Dean glares at me but turns and leaves the train car. Thomas follows after him to make the phone call, and I run back toward the sleeper cars.

I stop first at cabin thirteen. No luck. It's locked solid, won't even budge. Realizing I don't have time for this, I race through to the next car where I find cabin twenty-seven. The door is shut, but when I touch the handle, it moves. Stepping back, I take my gun from my holster, cock it, and hold it ready. Positioning myself so I'm not directly in front of the door, I slide it open.

It's only one of the tiny compartments designed for one person or an extraordinarily cozy couple to travel in, so there's little room for anyone to hide. I still step inside and look in every corner. That's when I notice there are belongings there. A pair of shoes sits in one corner. A bag is stuffed on a shelf. On the small sill in front of the window is a scattering of change and what looks like a plastic-coated chain with a small lock attached, complete with a couple of keys. This must be what the man left behind when he stepped off the train. I glance around again and immediately notice I don't see a wallet.

Footsteps coming down the car bring me back to the door, my gun poised. Thomas stops several feet away from me, his eyes wide.

"Cabin ten," he tells me. "The passenger who was supposed to be on this train is on the other one. He booked a new ticket and is in cabin ten."

I take out my phone and call Sam as I walk past Thomas back to cabin thirteen.

"You need to go to cabin ten," I tell him. "You need to get inside. The passenger who got off this train and delayed it is supposedly in there."

"On it," Sam says.

"I'm going to cabin thirteen. We only have about ten minutes to figure this out," I tell him.

Just for good measure, I try the door on cabin thirteen again, but it doesn't budge.

"It's locked from the inside," Thomas says. "There's a latch. It's the only thing that would hold it closed."

"Is this cabin bigger than the last one?" I ask.

"Yes, it's a full bedroom."

"Good. That gives me some room to work with."

"What do you mean?" he asks.

I step back and steady myself. "Back up."

I back up against the wall behind me for stability, then lift my leg and shove my whole weight onto the lock. The heavy sound echoes loudly through the car, but I don't care anymore. There's no time for subtlety.

"Can't you use your gun?" the conductor asks.

"Not unless you want to risk either shooting through whoever is in this room, or having the bullet bounce back into you," I tell him.

I give the door another kick. This time, it makes a popping sound. One more cracks it enough to slide slightly open, revealing the latch. It's hanging, and I smash the butt of my gun into it until it falls the rest of the way off.

"Or you could do that," Thomas nods.

I push the door the rest of the way open, and beside me, Thomas gasps. Sprawled on the bed is a dark-haired woman wearing the same uniform as Thomas. Her hand hangs from the side of the bed, a metal box attached around her wrist.

"Out of curiosity, Thomas, what's Miranda's last name?"

"Parsons," he says. "Why?"

"Of course," I mutter under my breath. My phone rings, and I answer as I press my fingers to Miranda's neck.

Sam's face swims into focus. "Emma, I think I found what we were looking for."

The camera turns to reveal a man sitting in a blue recliner beside a window, strapped to the back around his head, shoulders, and torso. His legs are bound in front of him. He's unconscious, but his arms have been wrapped around a box and secured.

"It's ticking."

CHAPTER FORTY-FIVE

GREG

TWO YEARS AGO...

Greg walked out of his office and headed down the hallway. It was a long day, and he was looking forward to dinner. A few doors down, he paused and rapped on the partially open door.

"Come on in," Emma called from inside.

He leaned around to poke his head in and smiled at her.

"Ready to go?" he asked.

"Almost," she said. "I'm just finishing up a few things."

"You're still working?" he asked. "Do you realize what time it is?"

She tilted the phone beside her up so she could look at the screen.

"Three minutes after everybody else got off for the day?"

"Exactly. Come on. It's time for dinner."

"Greg, I have a few things I have to finish up. It's not going to be the end of the world if you don't eat at exactly the right time. Just come in and sit down. I'll be done in a minute," she said. "You can look over the menu and decide what you want."

"I already know what I want," he said.

"Of course you do," she muttered through a sigh.

"What's that supposed to mean?" he frowned.

She shook her head as she checked over another sheet of paper and tucked it into a folder that she shoved across her desk.

"Nothing," she said.

"Obviously, it means something. You know that I like to keep a schedule," he pointed out.

"Yes, I do," she said. "I have ever since I've known you."

"Then, what's the problem? I don't understand why you're upset."

"I'm not upset," said Emma. She cocked her head for a moment as if considering something. "No, actually, I am upset. Yes, I've known you liked your schedule for a long time. It's one of the things I found kind of endearing and quirky about you. It's just... it's like the six months I didn't eat anything but coconut granola for breakfast."

"That wasn't a quirk. It was a habit," Greg protested.

"It was. One that I really enjoyed and that made me feel like my day had gotten off to a good start. And then one morning you invited me to come with you to your usual breakfast spot. Do you remember? It was after morning PT. The workout was especially hard that morning, and we were both sweaty and starving at the end of it."

"'Course I remember," he said. "I'd been watching you and was so impressed by you. I couldn't help but ask you to come with me. I'd been trying to figure out a way to ask you out for a year."

"And you finally did. And I said yes. And my granola sat in its little plastic baggie in my desk drawer until I had it for a snack later that afternoon."

"Are we just reminiscing about the beginning of our relationship? Because if we are, I'd really like to do it over dinner. If not, I'm not understanding the point."

Emma let out a sigh and slid another file over to the first.

"The point is, I delayed my granola for you. People shift. They adjust. They change. Routine is one thing, but that's all you are. You could, for once, be willing to not follow your routine for me."

"I thought you enjoyed going to dinner with me on Friday nights," Greg said.

"I do," Emma said, her shoulders sagging. "But can't you see I'm backstroking through case files right now? This investigation is taking up every second of my time. It's taking up seconds I don't even have yet. I'm going into default with Father Time. And all you care about is making sure you get to the same restaurant at the same time to sit at the same table and eat the same meal served by the same waitress as every Friday. You couldn't come in here and notice how busy I am and consider ordering takeout and hanging out here with me? Isn't that the point of having dinner with me? Having dinner... with me? Both of those things would be accomplished by sitting on my couch with a container of fried rice just as well as sitting across a table eating salmon. It might even be more fun."

Greg stared at her. He struggled to come up with what to say to her. Of course he wanted to spend time with her. They had been together for more than a year, and he thought they were getting to a point things were fairly serious. He'd even taken a few exploratory trips to jewelry stores. But it seemed recently she was pushing back against parts of their relationship. Parts of him. He liked things in order. He liked routine. That wasn't always an option considering his line of work, but whenever he had the ability to control what was around him, he did.

He looked at her across the desk and tried to understand what she was telling him. Finally, he nodded.

"Do you want me to go pick something up?" he asked.

She smiled. "Yes. Thank you."

"I'll be right back."

He stood and leaned over her desk to kiss her before walking out of the office. As he walked through the parking garage, a flicker of movement caught his attention. Someone had been standing at the corner of the building and ducked behind it when he walked out. Greg strode toward it, his hand moving to his hip automatically.

"Who's there?" he called out.

When there was no answer, he continued forward, releasing his weapon. He was still tense from a face-off with a trafficker only a few weeks before. He buried the nerves in his routine, holding back any emotion by staying in the same rhythm. It kept him steady. But he was thrown off now, and the back of his neck tingled as he swung around the corner, his gun poised.

The figure in front of him didn't flinch. He stood in the shadows, his hands by his sides, not reacting to Greg's weapon or to the tightness in his jaw. As the feeling of threat slid away, Greg was better able to focus on the man himself. He took a step forward, and more light touched his face. Greg shook his head, not believing what he was seeing.

Looking back at him was a face he thought he would never see again. The face was older. New lines by his eyes and a scar along the curve of his jaw. But it was him. He knew his eyes.

"Greg?"

"Yes," Greg answered.

"You do know who I am." It wasn't a question, but a confirmation. Greg only nodded. "Good. You'll have to forgive me for the unconventional way I went about meeting with you. I'm aware this is not in compliance with protocol, but I trust you'll understand why I can't be seen. You'll also understand if I ask for complete discretion."

"Of course."

"Thank you," he said, taking a step closer. "I'll be brief. I've spent the last several years deep undercover, investigating the weapons trade and its connection to human trafficking. I'm known only as Lotan now. Remember that. It will keep you safer."

Greg tucked his gun away as he shook his head in confusion.

"Keep me safer?" he frowned. "I don't understand."

"My mission is going exceptionally well. It's gaining tremendous ground, and the benefits could be enormous. But what's to come will be far more challenging than anything we've already faced. I've been sent to recruit the top elite agents to join the mission. You'll have to understand it will mean completely separating from your current life. You'll leave your home, your current role here. You'll have to end your relationship with Emma."

"Emma..." Greg gasped. "Does she..."

"She doesn't know, and it has to remain that way. Involving her could compromise the cover and safety of everyone involved. You've proven yourself, Greg. We've been watching you for some time, and we are extremely impressed by you. Would you be willing to discuss the details with me? Perhaps tomorrow?"

Greg nodded. "Yes. Absolutely. I am honored. Thank you, sir."

"Thank you. Please remember, this cannot be discussed with anyone."

"Of course."

"I will meet with you tomorrow and fill you in. Take tonight to consider whether you are ready for this type of assignment. If you are, you'll want to start separating yourself from your life now. Don't make any arrangements or leave any trace. But get your mind in order," Lotan said.

Greg nodded.

"I look forward to talking with you tomorrow."

CHAPTER FORTY-SIX

"We have to figure out how to disarm it," I say.

"Emma," Thomas says. "They're making announcements about the approach to the station. You only have a few minutes."

"Crap. Alright. Sam, show me the bomb," I say.

"Should we try to disconnect it from him?" Sam asks.

"No," I tell him. "Don't try to remove it. You have no idea how it's wired. Trying to take the tape away or moving his hands could trip it. We have to disarm it from where it is. I can't see all of the details. You have to tell me what it looks like. Do you see anything that might get you started?"

"No," Sam tells me. "It's just the box. It's exactly like you see it."

"Look around the room. Is there anything that stands out to you?" Something suddenly occurs to me. "His wallet. Do you see his wallet?"

"Yes. It's on the table," he tells me.

"Open it."

Sam picks up the thick black leather wallet and opens it.

"His ID. Credit cards. A membership card to a cigar club. I didn't even know that was a thing anymore. What am I looking for?" he asks.

"His ticket. Remember they said he didn't have a ticket to get on this train. That means he didn't buy his ticket online. He could have just pulled it up on his phone. But he left the physical one here," I suggest.

He reaches into the pocket and pulls out a train ticket that's been folded in half. He flips it over to reveal handwriting.

"'Tick tock, tick tock Emma,'" he reads. "This will be much worse than turning into a pumpkin."

"His watch," I say. "Is he wearing a watch?"

"Yes," Sam confirms.

"Turn it to midnight."

Without disrupting the tape, he carefully turns the dial on the side of the watch. As soon as it hits midnight, the crystal pops up, revealing a hidden compartment beneath the face.

"It's another note. 'Open the top and look inside.' The top of the bomb?"

"Yes. Do it," I answer breathlessly.

I can almost hear the seconds going by. The train is noticeably slower. Sam opens the top of the box and looks inside.

"Holy crap. I've never seen anything like this. I don't even know where to start."

"Show me," I tell him.

He holds the phone, so I can look into the box at the bomb. It's incredibly elaborate, with what looks like several incendiary devices connected into one system. On the side of the screen, I can see the top of the box. Something is written inside. Sam seems to see it at the same moment and picks it up.

"Some lines are red; some lines are blue. It's not going to be that easy for you," he reads.

"I am way less than amused by his poetry," I mutter. "Wait, show me the bomb again." He shows me the box, and I notice a purple line going down the middle. "The purple one. Can you cut the purple one?"

"Is that safe?" he asks. "He clearly wants us to cut the purple one. That's too obvious."

"I don't know, Sam. I'm not on the bomb squad. But at this point, it's either we try, or we wait for disaster. Which do you want to do?" I ask.

He takes a deep, shuddering breath. "We try."

"Do you have anything to cut it?"

"I don't have a knife or scissors." He looks around. "There's a pair of nail clippers."

"You're going to have to try it," I tell him.

He grabs the clippers and snips at the wire. I hold my breath. The clippers go through, and the wire slips away. It appears to have been holding a small hatch closed, and the metal piece opens as the wire releases. Sam gingerly pushes it over, revealing a keyhole.

"There's no key. I don't have a key," he says. "I don't see one anywhere in the room."

"Hold on," I tell him, taking off down the hallway to snatch the chain from the window in the other cabin. "It's a bike lock. That's seriously messed up."

"How is that key going to unlock this?" he asks.

"It won't. But it will unlock her." I try the first key in the box hanging from Miranda's arm. Thomas is sitting beside her, stroking her arm. "She's alive, Thomas. She's alive."

The first key doesn't work, and I scramble to try the second. It opens the box, and a thick piece of paper falls out. I unfold it.

"What is it?" Sam asks.

"I never told you my secret. My lips are locked up tight." I draw in a shuddering breath that rattles and aches in my lungs. "Sam, check his mouth."

"What?" Sam asks.

"His mouth!" The train whistle blares overhead, cutting through my words. "Open his mouth!"

Sam pulls down on the man's chin, revealing a piece of string coiled on his tongue. He tugs on it, drawing it out of the man's throat until a long, glistening key slides from his lips. Sam plunges it down into the hole, and the ticking stops.

I cry out in relief and tip from my knees to sit on the floor just as the train starts to pull into the station.

"Thomas, please go tell every conductor you can find to keep the passengers in their place. Don't let anyone off the train," I tell him.

"I'll call train security, so they'll get to the platform," Sam says.

"They're already there," I tell him. "I called them."

"You did?" Sam asks.

"Yes. And the police. After we found the woman. I didn't tell you because I didn't want you to be afraid," I tell him.

"Emma. You said this man keeps his promises. He said no police."

"I know. But we couldn't do this on our own. That's something I'm trying to learn," I tell him.

"You did the right thing."

The train stops as I walk into the empty train car to stay with the first body until the police can come secure the scene. I sit down beside my suitcase and look out the window at the sunlight streaming down. Police and confused passengers swarm the platform, a stark contrast to the serene sky above them. I lift my eyes, just for a minute, and pretend it isn't there.

The door opens, and Dean Steele walks in. My shoulders tense.

"I told you not to come back here," I round on him. "This is a secure scene, and you need to leave."

Thomas steps up behind him, three police officers following close behind.

"Agent Emma, we need to talk," Dean says.

"You're right. We do. Starting with why you took my computer out of its bag."

He looks stung. "You knew it was me?"

"Of course I did. I believed you about the woman, you know. But those are the only words out of your mouth I'll ever believe. I don't know who you are, but you need to stay away from me. But first, you can explain to the officers how you got the seat note belonging to a dead man to put it on my computer screen," I say.

"I didn't do that," he says. "I opened your computer, but I went back to my seat before I could even guess your password."

"Because I came," Thomas admits.

"Thomas... you?" I ask.

He nods. "I put the note on your screen. It was sitting on the seat beside yours when I walked by, and I didn't want it to get lost. I was too embarrassed to mention it to you, and then I completely forgot in the situation."

Something catches his attention out the window, and his head snaps over to look. "Oh, my god. It's Mr. Jones."

I follow his gaze and see the man who sat across the aisle from me being led away from the train in handcuffs. In that moment it hits me we hadn't found him. As soon as we found Miranda, I was so swept up in disarming the bomb I didn't think about him still being missing.

"Excuse me," I say, pushing past the group at the door. Another officer tries to block me from getting out, but I reach into my pocket and take out my card holder, showing him my badge. "FBI. I'm the one who called."

He steps out of the way, and I jump down, running after the arresting officers.

"Excuse me," I call until they turn around. "Emma Griffin, FBI. I called about this. What's going on here?"

"We've placed this man under arrest for suspicion of murder and terroristic acts. I'm sure it doesn't surprise you that there will likely be several other charges," one of the officers says with a self-fulfilled smile.

Mr. Jones sways slightly, unstable on his feet.

"What surprises me is that you're arresting him. He is not responsible for this," I say.

"We found significant evidence in his personal belongings linking him to these crimes."

"Significant evidence? How?" I ask incredulously. "The investigation has barely started." He sways again, and I gesture at him. "This man is clearly compromised."

"We believe he tried to commit suicide. He was found in an overhead luggage compartment, heavily sedated."

"And you think he just climbed right up there himself?" I ask.

"Right now, that's what the evidence says."

The officers move around me, half-dragging the man toward a nearby car. I call Sam to tell him what happened.

"He didn't do it, Sam. He couldn't have. Not only does he have no connection to me, but he wasn't on the train long enough. And he wasn't on your train. I don't know what evidence they supposedly found, but somebody planted it," I say.

"They'll investigate, Emma. We will work this out."

"And until then?" I ask.

"What do you mean?"

"We still have no idea who did this. Two people are dead, Sam. Because of me," I say.

"It isn't your fault, Emma. You didn't do anything wrong."

"But it will keep happening. And as long as they have that man in custody, the investigation is going to be skewed."

"What are you saying?" he asks.

"I keep searching. I go wherever I have to go to find the answers."

"I'll be there soon."

The next hour is a constant stream of police and questions. I tell them everything. I retrace my steps. I watch as they photograph and record the bodies. It will take time before they are able to be moved, but at least the crime scene investigators cover them, offering them some of the dignity so horribly taken from them. It feels like it stretches on forever before Sam finally arrives and takes me in his arms.

"I love you," he whispers.

"I love you, too."

CHAPTER FORTY-SEVEN

HIM

He stared at the screen; his heart pounding so hard in his chest; it felt like his ribs were going to crack. The reporter walked up and down the train platform in her ridiculous heels, caring more about the way her hair flipped over her shoulder than what was going on around her. Emma was no more than five feet away. Her arms wrapped around her body. Her hair tangled at the base of her neck. Her face drawn. Two officers stood beside her, peppering her with questions. And that sheriff. That useless sheriff. He stood right there and did nothing to protect her.

They were doing nothing. She was standing there out among all the others as if she was like them. As if they were equals to her.

Listening to everything she went through made his blood boil. How could this happen? How could anything like this happen on his watch? Who could dare to threaten her, to disrespect him in such a grievous way?

The reporter paced several feet in the opposite direction. The camera turned to pan over the train as a dull voice gave a brief, sanitized overview of the horrors that happened inside. Less than two hours before, not even long enough for all the passengers to have been let out, Emma led police officers to two brutalized bodies and handed over evidence of the harrowing ride she was forced to endure. They weren't releasing everything. It was far too graphic, they noted, but there were also details the investigators wanted to keep concealed as part of their investigation.

But he knew. Even the brief details they would report told him this was targeted. This wasn't a random event. A spontaneous bout of violence made all the more gruesome by its setting. No, whoever planned this specifically had Emma in mind. She was the one they wanted to torment. It brought her close to death.

He couldn't stand for this. This could not be the way it was. For years he had been working. Quietly building. Biding his time and forcing himself not to act too quickly. He knew how important it was to be ready and ensure she was, too. He always told himself it was going to be a major adjustment for her. It wasn't going to be just a simple change, a fast and easy transition. As much as he would love for that to happen—for her to just feel the connection and know her place—it wasn't going to be like that. It was up to him to show her the way. It was up to him to make sure he had a life provided for her so she would know just how precious, just how important she was.

How precious and important she had always been.

He had a lot of time to make up for. A lot of things missed, for which he had no choice. She didn't know that. She didn't know what kept them apart, and he wanted to be able to show that to her. The life he was creating was what she deserved. It was what she was worth.

He thought there were still things he needed to do. There were still tasks to complete and preparations to be made. But he couldn't wait anymore. This was the breaking point. This changed everything. There was someone threatening Emma. He couldn't allow that to happen. He couldn't allow her to be ripped away from him.

It would be a different kind of pain than what he already went through. He knew that. Nothing would ever compare to what it was like the night he lost Mariya. His love for Emma was obviously different. But he couldn't suffer that again.

Everything had to change. It was time for him to take drastic measures. His plans had always included showing her how misled she had been in her life and proving he was her truth. When she saw the reality of what she always knew, the real faces behind the masks she had come to know and love, it would horrify her. It would be hard. He didn't look forward to causing her that type of pain and devastation. But the beauty that would come of it would be far worth it.

There was only one thing he could do. One step he could take to open her eyes and start to guide her out of her life of danger and loss, and into her position of glory. It would be brutal, but the thought had always been in the back of his mind that it would come to this.

The time had come to sacrifice the Lamb.

CHAPTER FORTY-EIGHT

I t became clear pretty quickly that Sam and I were not going to be allowed to leave the area for a while. I wouldn't go so far as to say the investigators actually believe we were involved, but they also aren't leaping to our unwavering defense, either. That doesn't particularly surprise me. But it wasn't particularly pleasant after the day I just faced.

Sam and I sit in the police station, hands wrapped around Styrofoam cups of terrible coffee. Paper plates hold a few pastries neither of us have any interest in eating. We've been sitting in the same room for three hours, and no one has come to talk to us. Whether that's because of the incredible backup of people they're going to have to interview or a strategic plan, is yet to be revealed. Sam holds my hand, his thumb stroking the back of it. He doesn't need to say anything. I don't want him to say anything. There are no words either of us could offer the other one that would mean any more than just being able to sit there together.

Finally, the door opens, and two detectives walk in. One tosses a small stack of file folders onto the table before unbuttoning his jacket. I stare at the folders and lift my eyes to him.

"I'm not sure that was entirely necessary," I comment.

He shrugs and drops down into the chair across from us. The other officer walks over and extends his hand.

"Detective James Mayfield," he introduces himself as Sam takes his hand and shakes it.

"Sheriff Sam Johnson," he says. "Sherwood County."

Detective Mayfield nods and turns his attention to me.

"And, of course, I know who you are, Agent Griffin. Detective James Mayfield."

"Hi, Detective," I say, shaking his hand.

I don't like the way he says 'of course he knows who I am'. Not that it's all that out of the question. I've had my fair share of news features and interviews on the local news ever since my case in Feathered Nest. But he didn't address me in a professional capacity like I was an associate. Instead, there was a hint of being starstruck that makes me squirm. Especially when I look over at the other detective and see the disgust in his eyes. We have good cop, bad cop out in full force. I'm kind of interested to see how much of it is genuine and how much is contrived.

"'Course ya do," the other detective says snidely. "Everyone knows the famous Emma Griffin."

My eyes swing over to him again.

"And you are?"

"Detective Steven Legends," he grunts, his heavy accent in full force. "I'll be headin' up this investigation."

"Best of luck with it," I say.

Sam slides his eyes over to me. Even though I don't look at him, I can feel the disapproval.

"That s'posed to mean somethin'?" Detective Legends asks.

I mimic back the shrug he gave me when he first came in.

"Exactly what I said. Best of luck with it. It's not going to be easy," I tell him earnestly.

"Y'know Miss Griffin, investigators tend to not appreciate when people uncover crimes and don't immediately report them," he says.

"Agent Griffin, Detective. I'm well aware of that."

"As I'm sure you're aware, we especially don't take kindly to mishandled situations like that when they involve the lives of hundreds of other people," he says.

"Mishandled?" I ask. "Tell me, Detective. Were they mishandled because the decision was made to manage an unstable, dangerous situation with the best resources we had in that moment or was it mishandled because I'm the one who did it?"

"Of course not," Detective Mayfield cuts in. "That's not what he means. Of course, we are well aware of your prestigious accomplishments in the Bureau."

"That don't give her the right to break the law and put people's lives at risk. The FBI does not have authority over police. Just because she works for the Bureau doesn't mean she supersedes our department."

"I never said that I did," I defend myself. "I'm well aware the Bureau has limitations, and in my work, I understand the importance of cooperation with local law enforcement. But unless the jurisdictions around here are enormous, that train passed through several of them during that escape room from hell. I'll also remind you I did have the full cooperation of a police officer the entire time. So if it's simply my badge that bothers you, that should help you to rest a little easier."

"Would you have rather she called immediately and created even greater risk for every passenger on those trains? Every cop knows you advocate self-protection and the protection of others, acting in the best interest of other people around you regardless of the situation. Even if that means cooperating with a criminal to reduce danger. Hand over your wallet. Give them your PIN code. Don't taunt the man with a gun," Sam adds. "We had credible reason to believe that our decision was the only way we could have stopped it."

"Well, had ya called as soon as the first body was discovered, the trains coulda been diverted, and a proper investigation coulda started immediately."

"Which would have been a delightful process, had both trains been blown to smithereens," I bite back. I know it's part of a ploy, but this dude is getting on my nerves.

"You have no idea if that would have actually happened," the detective says. "A lot of people threaten things, Agent Griffin. That don't mean they have the ability to actually make them happen."

"I'm well aware of that. But I'm also well aware of the human capacity for evil. Likely far more than you are. Cruelty is unfortunately not a rare trait, and I'm not going to be the one to eat the poison M & M."

"'Scuse me?" he asks.

"If you had a bowl of M & M candies, and I tossed in several that were dipped in poison, would you still be comfortable eating a handful?"

Detective Legends looks up at Detective Mayfield, then back at me.

"I wouldn't," Mayfield notes.

Legends merely shrugs an agreement.

"The point is, all the threats and risks you encounter during your career aren't going to come to fruition. There are going to be failed attempts, self-important criminals talking out of their asses, and ones you managed to thwart. Sure, the vast majority of the M & M's are going to be fine. But do you take that chance? Because the poison is there. It's real. Someone will threaten violence and go through with it. Someone will say 'I'm going to kill you' to someone in their life and not mean it as a euphemism," I explain.

"Ma'am, I'm well aware that threats—"

I raise a hand to cut him off.

"You might not like what happened on that train, but I don't regret how I handled it. Not for one minute. I did exactly what I needed to do when I needed to do it, and thanks to my work, almost everyone on both of those trains is still alive. There are few other people on this Earth who would understand that. Maybe none at all. Until you have stood in the place I have and gone through the same things, you will never grasp what it's like. It's easy to sit by and think maybe you'd have done it better if I'd just followed procedure. If I'd just done it your way. But that's not the way it works. This situation was about me more than it was about anyone else. It was my responsibility to do everything in my power to bring it to as safe a conclusion as possible. You don't know what you're up against here, Detective," I tell him.

"Which is why we need your help," Detective Mayfield says. "You're going to need to give us insight as we investigate what happened and bring the perp to justice."

"There are very few things I want more than for that to happen," I tell him.

———

It's another two hours before they finally let Sam and me leave. They've asked us to stay close by, rather than continuing on to Feathered Nest or going home to Sherwood. In these first few days of the investigation, having us close will be instrumental in their progress. I don't tell them they are coming in for just one battle of a war. They will learn that soon enough.

"Oh," I mention to Sam as I finally strip out of my clothes and step under a hot shower. "You didn't tell me if you got in touch with Clancy."

"I did," he calls in from the front of the hotel room. "It turns out Marren isn't in town at all. She left a few days ago to visit her sister."

"I didn't even know she had a sister," I say.

"Apparently, not many people do. They aren't close, but since they're both getting on in years, they've been trying to reconnect. Clancy says he talked to her about it the day before she left."

"And that was a few days ago? Like after I got the train ticket?"

"Sounds like it," Sam says. "I thought you had already come to the conclusion she didn't send it to you though."

"No, I did. She obviously isn't the one who sent me on that train. What I'm wondering is, why did LaRoche not mention she was leaving? He went to check on her. Wouldn't he have mentioned I said I was coming in?"

"I don't know. But that's not something for you to worry about right now. Tonight, you rest."

I go to sleep that night happy to be in Sam's arms, but feeling like I'm still on the train. Barreling forward with no idea where I'm going to stop.

CHAPTER FORTY-NINE

Two days later, Sam and I walk out of the police station and head back toward our hotel. The last forty-eight hours have been both a blur and incredibly tedious. The hours melded together as I went over page after page of evidence, told the same story over and over again. I couldn't tell if they were waiting for me to make a mistake, or if the details were just so unbelievable, they had to hear it again. I had no difficulty repeating myself as many times as they needed me to. Those images are seared into my mind. They aren't going anywhere, and I will be able to recount those details for the rest of my life.

Little progress has been made in the case, which doesn't surprise me. But it does infuriate me. They still haven't released Mr. Jones, whose first name I learned is Mason. The evidence they have against him is shaky, to say the least. Traces of blood in his luggage. Fingerprints in places on the train where he shouldn't have been. Of course, I know why those fingerprints are there. He has been all over that train in places he shouldn't be.

At least Miranda Parsons regained consciousness today. She explained that she and Mason had already met up when she got the first call about the passenger who got off the train. When she finally noticed it ten minutes later, she hurried to meet him, and there was a man there. He said he was supposed to be on the sleeper car but wanted one more cigarette before the train took off, and in his haste, he forgot his tickets and identification.

Miranda was so embarrassed by her lapse in professionalism that she didn't question the passenger. She got his ID for him and had the redcaps put a piece of luggage in the baggage car that she thought was his because it was sitting next to him. She would find his ticket to board, she promised. It took two men to lift the bike box into the car. When he walked away because she didn't get back to him right away, the conductor decided to get going.

As of now, we still don't know exactly the series of events. We know the blonde woman, Anna Strayer, was on the platform that morning but didn't get onto the train alive. Sometime between the original passenger getting off the train and the train starting, someone murdered a man named Andrew Price and left his body for me to find.

It's Miranda and the original passenger, Kelly Barden, that I keep bringing up when we talk about Mason Jones. Miranda was in a passenger car locked from the inside, while Kelly was strapped to a seat of a different train with a bomb in his lap. There is no way that Mason could have been on both trains at once. I think I got through to them today. I have no doubt that by tomorrow he'll be released. It will be a celebration for him, but they'll still have questions hanging over us. Hanging over me.

It's going to be harder to chase the answers now. Within an hour of getting off the train, I tried to show the police the Catch Me profile, but it had been wiped. Everything was deleted. With the word of everyone who saw it, including Bellamy and Eric, the police know it did exist and what it had on it. But we can't use it for any more digging.

The profile isn't the only thing that disappeared in the earliest moments of the investigation. Dean Steele was nowhere to be found. Somehow, despite the officers positioned along the train, despite the barriers put up to carefully herd passengers through the phases of questions and checks and on into the station, he slipped away without anyone noticing. He hasn't shown up for an interview. And when I looked back to where I remembered first seeing his name, listed among the comments on a few of Mary's videos, they, too, were gone.

It's frustrating, but I've overcome worse. It won't stop me.

We get to the hotel, and as we step into the elevator, Sam turns to me.

"Emma, I have to ask you something."

"What is it?" I asked.

"It's about your birthday," he says.

I let out a sigh and hang my head, shaking it. I don't want to have this conversation. I've had to talk about it too many times already, and I don't want to do it again. Not with him. Not with all the knowledge he has.

"You didn't tell them about the discrepancy in the date," he says. "You left it out when telling the police about the clues."

"I guess I did," I admit. "It didn't really make much sense to tell them."

"Why not?" he asks. "Isn't that part of the evidence? Shouldn't that be part of the investigation?"

"Why?" I ask. "Are they going to do a poll and see how many people say my birthday is the twenty-second as opposed to the twenty-third?"

"You know the answer to that question, Emma. You said it yourself."

"Sam, don't."

"You've already told me twice before that you think you saw your father following you. That he was in Sherwood walking down the sidewalk and then again near Quantico. I need you to tell me honestly if you think there is any chance this could be your father."

I grit my teeth against the tears burning in the backs of my eyes and the pain searing down my chest.

"No," I tell him. "I don't."

"Why?" he asks.

"Because if there is one thing my father never did, it's lie to me. He might have done a lot of things that I don't understand and has probably done a lot of things I don't know about. But that is one I can tell you without a doubt. This wasn't my father, Sam. I know that's not much of an argument. It's not a defense. But I feel it in my bones. This couldn't have been him."

"Then how would they know those things about you?" he asks.

"I don't know. That's part of it. Don't you see? The details were there, but they didn't make sense. Those weren't my father trying to speak to me. They were someone trying to speak for my father."

The phone in the room is ringing when we get in; Sam rushes over to pick it up.

"Sorry," he says. "We've had our phones silenced while we were in the police station. Do you want to talk to— " his voice stops, and his eyes lift to me. "We'll be there as soon as we can."

He hangs up the phone, and I walk toward him.

"Who was that? Where are we going to be as soon as we can?" I ask.

"Emma, sit down," he says.

I perch on the end of the bed, staring at him.

"Sam, what is it? What's going on?"

"That was Eric. He was calling from the hospital," he says.

"The hospital? What's going on? Is it Bellamy? What happened to her?"

I try to stand up, to start packing my bags, but he takes me by the shoulders and eases me back down.

"Bellamy's fine. It's not her. It's Greg."

I feel like I can't breathe for a few seconds. Sam takes a step toward me, and I hold up my hand to stop him.

"Greg?" I gasp. "He came back?"

"They found him," Sam tells me. "In the front yard of your house."

"Is he...?"

"He's alive. But just barely. Eric didn't get into too many details. But apparently, it's pretty bad. He is in a coma right now. They want to keep him under for a while to let his body heal."

Sam looks down at his phone and presses a few buttons, swiping across the screen as if he's looking at something.

"What's that?" I asked.

He opens his mouth as if to say something, but no sound comes out. He swallows hard and comes to sit down beside me.

"Emma, when they found him, he was wrapped in plastic, and there were papers with him. They haven't released everything yet, but there were some pictures. This is one of them."

He turns the phone screen to me. It feels like the world has crashed in on itself. Black dots dance in front of my eyes, and my stomach surges up into my throat. I gasp for breath and Sam reaches to take the phone from me. But I clamp my hand around it, and I won't let it go. It's excruciating to look at the picture, but I can't stop.

The image seems to be from a security or surveillance camera of some kind. Not one of the grainy black-and-white ones that take the choppy time-lapse images. But one that shows full detail. Bright color. Bright enough to see the flash of Greg's watch on his wrist and the color of my father's eyes.

"Emma, are you all right?" he asks. "I know you just told me..."

"Sam..."

The shock is wearing off, and I'm looking at the picture closer now. Something is standing out to me; it makes my hands burn, and my lungs incapable of holding air.

"I know what you're going to say, but please listen to me. This picture is real and..."

"Sam, I know it's real. But I need you to listen to me. My father has a scar on his face," I say.

"I know. I remember. Here, you can see it," he says, tracing his finger along the faint line curving over a strong jaw.

I shake my head.

"No. Sam, remember. Think about it. Think about when he got that scar. We weren't very old. Maybe ten. It was one of the very few times I got to spend part of fall in Sherwood. Don't you remember that?"

"It was a long time ago, Emma."

"I know it was. But try to think. My father was helping the neighbor across the street. The one who used to live in the house where Janet and Paul live now. He used to mow their lawn for them because they were old. But he mowed over a beer bottle some kid had tossed into their backyard. It shattered, and a piece of glass cut his face. It almost cut his eye, Sam. The scar on my father's face is across his cheekbone. Not his jaw."

"He's been gone a long time. He could have got another scar in that time," Sam says.

"He could have. Of course, he could have. But you can see both sides of his face in this picture. Whoever this is, he doesn't have a scar on his cheekbone. He's been gone a long time, but that cut was far too deep for the scar to completely disappear. Do you remember the picture of what I thought was my mother and father, but the initials were wrong? It should have said M and I, but I know it said M and J."

"What are you saying, Emma?"

"The birth certificate we found from when my father was delivered by the midwives in Iowa. It wasn't wrong. That mark wasn't in the wrong place. They didn't miss when they tried to mark a single birth. They marked a multiple birth."

EPILOGUE

It takes a while for me to calm down enough to even think clearly, much less bring myself to pick up my phone. Bellamy answers on the first ring.

"Are you alright?" she asks.

"No," I tell her. "Not really. I know this is going to sound callous of me, but I can't come there right now. I appreciate you being there, and it means a lot to have you and Eric with him, but I can't come to the hospital right now."

"No, Emma, that doesn't sound callous. This is a lot to hit you with. And you've had a really rough few days. Take your time with it. He is not conscious, and he has no idea we're here, probably. Of course, I say that and watch him be listening to me right now."

She lets out a forced laugh, but I can't reciprocate it.

"You don't need to stay with him all the time or anything. But if you could just update me and let me know how things are progressing. I will come. I'll get there."

"I know you will," she says.

"B, about that picture..."

I get up and walk over to the window. It's not a beautiful view by any means. It looks out over the parking lot, but it's something other than the inside of the room that feels like it's closing in on me.

"His scar," she says, and I draw in a sharp breath.

"You saw it," I say.

"I've looked at your father's picture so many times I feel like I know him. I haven't said anything," she says, her voice lowering to a murmur.

"Don't," I tell her. "Not yet."

I start to tell her more about the train as I pull aside the curtain, but looking down at the parking lot stops me.

"Emma?" she says. "Are you still there?"

"Sam," I call over. "Come here."

"Emma," Bellamy says. "What's going on?"

"B, I'll call you back. Forget what I just said. Stay with Greg. As much as you can. Stay with him."

Sam steps up beside me and looks down at the parking lot. From this angle, we can see the car we rented yesterday, so we don't feel so stranded. The late-afternoon sunlight shines down on the simple, generic sedan, making the large, dark bouquet of flowers stand out against the silver.

Without saying anything, Sam and I bolt out of the room. Not bothering to wait for the elevator, we scramble down the steps and out through the side exit. The emergency alarm screams behind us, but neither of us care. I can't breathe as I walk toward the car. Sitting on the hood of the car is a massive bouquet of roses with petals so dark they nearly match the black velvet ribbon wrapped around their stems.

A cream cardstock envelope nestled among the blooms has my name written across it in the color of rust. I open the envelope and pull out a piece of matching stationery. The top corner of the note has today's date. As the handwriting flows down the page, it changes from the block letters of the cards in the train to the script of the note that came with the train ticket.

It's rude to ignore an invitation, Emma.

You should have come when you were asked.
Didn't your mother teach you better manners?
Do you want to know what happened to her?
I know a secret.
Come see me.

P.S. Jake sends his regards

THE END

I hope you enjoyed this fifth book in the Emma Griffin series. I appreciate your continued support! No worries if this is the first book you read, all the paperbacks are available at Amazon.com and most online retailers.

If you enjoyed this book, please leave me a review on Amazon! Your reviews allow me to get the validation to keep this series going and also helps attract new readers.
Just a moment of your time is all that is needed.

I promise to always do my best to bring you thrilling adventures.

Yours,
A.J. Rivers

P.S. Be sure to checkout The Girl and the Deadly Express, Emma's next mystery. You will have some answers to the questions you've been wondering about in the series!

P.S.S. If for some reason you didn't like this book or found typos or other errors, please let me know personally. I do my best to read and respond to every email at aj@riversthrillers.com

STAYING IN TOUCH WITH A.J.

Type the link below in your internet browser now to join my mailing list and get your free copy of Edge Of The Woods.

https://dl.bookfunnel.com/ze03jzd3e4

MORE EMMA GRIFFIN FBI MYSTERIES

Emma Griffin's FBI Mysteries is the new addictive best-selling series by A.J. Rivers. Make sure to get them all below!

Visit my author page on Amazon to order your missing copies now! Now available in paperback!

ALSO BY A.J. RIVERS

The Girl and the Deadly End

The Girl and the Hunt

The Girl and the Deadly Express

The Girl Next Door

The Girl in the Manor

The Girl That Vanished

The Girl in Cabin 13

Gone Woman